THE RED TAPE MURDERS

Superintendent Budd's latest murder investigation begins with the murder of a solicitor, found strangled with red tape. Soon, two more local solicitors are murdered in similar fashion. Eventually Budd learns that two years earlier, a man shot himself when about to lose the bungalow he built, under a compulsory purchase order of the council. Two of the solicitors had acted in the sale of the land, and the third had acted for the council. Is someone seeking vengeance for the man who committed suicide — himself a victim of red tape?

GERALD VERNER

THE RED TAPE MURDERS

Complete and Unabridged

LINFORD
Leicester

First published in Great Britain

First Linford Edition
published 2018

A catalogue record for this book is available
from the British Library.

ISBN 978–1–4448–3797–1

Published by
F. A. Thorpe (Publishing)
Anstey, Leicestershire

Set by Words & Graphics Ltd.
Anstey, Leicestershire
Printed and bound in Great Britain by
T. J. International Ltd., Padstow, Cornwall

This book is printed on acid-free paper

1

Miss Catkin looked at her watch and experienced a shock of apprehension. When she had looked at it before, it had shown the time to be half-past three. It *still* showed the time to be half-past three.

Miss Catkin held the watch to her ear. There was no reassuring tick. The watch had stopped!

She rose hurriedly from her desk and went into the outer office. Old Timothy Smithson, the managing clerk, was peering through his spectacles at a lease. His lips moved as he read, one of his habits that always annoyed Miss Catkin. This afternoon, however, she was too worried to even notice it.

'Mr. Smithson,' she said anxiously, 'what's the time?'

The old man laid down the document and looked at her over the top of his glasses. 'The — er — time, Miss Catkin?' he asked. 'Did you say the time?'

'Yes, the time,' said Miss Catkin impatiently. 'What is it? My watch has stopped.'

With exasperating deliberation, Mr. Smithson produced from his waistcoat pocket a large gold watch attached to a gold chain. Pressing the spring that opened the case, he consulted the dial. 'It's exactly four and a quarter minutes past four,' he announced.

'Oh, dear!' exclaimed Miss Catkin. 'Mr. Humphrey will be furious.' She almost ran to a small cupboard-like compartment, opening off the outer office, in which, among a number of other things, was housed a decrepit gas stove. Hastily she seized a kettle and filled it from the tap above a small sink. Banging it down on the stove, she felt on the shelf at the side for the box of matches that should have been there. But it wasn't.

'Oh, dear!' she said again. 'Really, *everything* is going wrong.'

She went back to the outer office. 'Have you a box of matches, Mr. Smithson?' she asked.

Mr. Smithson, deeply engrossed again

in his lease, looked up rather irritably. 'What *is* the matter, Miss Catkin?' he demanded. 'I'm extremely busy.'

'I'm sorry, but I must have some matches. The box on the little shelf by the stove isn't there.'

'You should check these things.' He fumbled in the outer pocket of his alpaca jacket, found a box of matches, and held them out to her. 'Please, let me have them back,' he said.

Miss Catkin rushed back to the cupboard-like compartment and lit the gas under the kettle. Why, she thought, did they put up with this antiquated arrangement? Why couldn't they buy an electric kettle? Possibly, it was because they liked being old-fashioned and out of date. Everything about the offices of Gamble, Chalkit, Gamble and Gamble was out of date. The furniture was dingy, the carpets threadbare and frayed, the typewriters ancient models that still typed but were always going wrong, the filing cabinets with wooden drawers that always stuck, and the quantity of dusty documents tied with faded red tape, stuffed in corners and piled on every available shelf.

Miss Catkin set out the cups and saucers and spoons on a wooden tray, put a dozen lumps of sugar in a china basin, and washed out the teapot. From the tin caddy, she measured out the usual quantity of tea. Would the kettle *never* boil?

Mr. Humphrey Gamble was very particular about his afternoon tea. It had to be made exactly as he liked it, and served with two digestive biscuits at precisely four o'clock each afternoon.

Well, he wouldn't get it today at four o'clock, thought Miss Catkin as she put the digestive biscuits on a small plate. There would be trouble about that. Mr. Humphrey's rather cold grey eyes would bore into her as he inquired, quite politely, but with a distinctly unpleasant intonation in his pedantic voice, the reason why his tea was late.

Miss Catkin pushed back a wisp of grey hair that had fallen over her forehead and stared at the kettle as though by the very intensity of her gaze she would force it to boil more quickly. Whether this had any effect or not is doubtful, but at last steam gushed from the spout, and spurts of water splashed over the stove.

She picked up the kettle-holder, grasped the handle of the kettle, and poured water into the teapot. Then she stirred the brewing tea vigorously with a spoon and poured some of it into a cup. She realized at once that in her agitation, she had forgotten the milk. Perhaps Mr. Humphrey wouldn't notice that the milk hadn't been put in first.

She added the milk, put the cup of tea, the sugar, and the plate of biscuits on a small tray, and carried it through the outer office to the door of Mr. Humphrey's room, watched by the disapproving eyes of the managing clerk. With a certain amount of trepidation, she knocked. The dispassionate voice of Mr. Humphrey Gamble, inviting her to come in, reached her ears faintly from the other side of the door. Apprehensively, she did so.

Mr. Humphrey Gamble was seated behind his large writing-table surrounded by piles of dingy documents, like an island in a paper sea. He was a thin man with stooping shoulders and a long bony nose. His hair, what there was of it, was grey, and his eyes lurked in hollows beneath bushy brows that were almost white.

As Miss Catkin put the tray down beside him, he looked ostentatiously at his watch. 'It appears to be twenty minutes past four, Miss Catkin,' he remarked.

'I'm very sorry, Mr. Humphrey,' she apologised a little flustered. 'I made a mistake in the time.'

'Punctuality,' said Mr. Gamble, 'is extremely important. In these slipshod days, I'm afraid its importance is apt to be overlooked.'

'Something went wrong with my watch,' explained Miss Catkin unhappily. 'I don't know *what* can be the matter with it.'

'That's most unfortunate,' said Mr. Gamble. 'I trust that you'll take steps to see that such a contingency does not happen again.'

'Oh, I will — indeed, I will!' declared

Miss Catkin. 'I really am so *very* sorry, Mr. Humphrey.'

Mr. Gamble inclined his head. Stretching out a thin and well-manicured hand, he delicately selected a lump of sugar and dropped it into his cup of tea. 'Very well. I shall be leaving a quarter of an hour earlier this evening — that is, at a quarter to six. I should like my letters ready for me to sign by half-past five, if you please.'

Miss Catkin withdrew with an inward sigh of relief. She gave Mr. Smithson his tea, hurriedly drank her own, and went back to her ancient typewriter. There were still quite a number of letters to do, and she would have all her work cut out to get them finished by five-thirty. She prayed that nothing would go wrong with the typewriter.

Mr. Humphrey Gamble drank his tea and ate his biscuits. He did both slowly, with the air of one performing a ritual. Mr. Gamble was a very orderly man. He lived to a timetable, taking a great deal of pleasure in doing certain things at a certain hour each day, and only varying his routine if business made it necessary.

He caught the same train every morning to bring him to town from his small house on the outskirts of London. He caught the same train every evening, with the exception of Saturdays and Sundays, to take him back again. That he should be leaving, this evening, a quarter of an hour earlier, was an unprecedented occurrence.

But it was a special occasion. It was his sister's birthday, and he was calling at a shop in the vicinity of his office to pick up a small gift that he had ordered for her. The shop closed at six, hence the reason for the necessity of leaving earlier than usual. Mr. Gamble had never married, and his sister looked after his house, cooked his meals, and saw that his well-ordered life ran smoothly.

Messrs. Gamble, Chalkit, Gamble and Gamble were a prosperous firm. They dealt mostly in property, nothing that could be remotely called exciting. Mr. Humphrey Gamble was the only surviving member of the firm. His father, Nathaniel Gamble, had died ten years previously. Mr. Gamble had considered, at that time, taking a partner but had decided against it, believing that he and Timothy Smithson, who had been with the firm since he was an articled clerk, could manage the business between them. Messrs. Gamble, Chalkit, Gamble and Gamble seldom indulged in litigation. Their business consisted for the most part in conveyancing, leases, the managing of estates, and similar matters that kept them out of the courts. They had one or two private clients whose affairs they handled, but they looked askance on general practice.

Mr. Gamble finished the perusal of an intricate valuation, locked the document away in the old-fashioned safe, and going to the private toilet that opened out of his office, carefully washed his hands. He came back just as Miss Catkin came in with the letters for his signature. He read them slowly, as was his custom, signed them, and gave them back to her to post.

'I shall be in at the usual time tomorrow morning,' he said as he put on his coat. 'I should be glad if you would start making three copies of the particulars concerning the Lattimer property. I shall require them after lunch.'

He passed through the outer office, wishing Timothy Smithson goodnight as he went out. It was a damp night but not, as yet, actually raining. Mr. Gamble called at the shop and picked up the present for his sister — a brooch with her initials in small pearls — and took a bus to the station. From the bookstall, he bought his usual evening paper, which he read during the comparatively short journey to his destination.

It was beginning to rain when he came out of the station where he lived. He glanced at the clock as he showed the ticket collector his season. It was five minutes to seven. He invariably dined at seven-thirty, after the glass of sherry which he, as invariably, took while his sister was putting the finishing touches to the meal.

The walk from the station to his house was not a very long one. It led through a rather secluded road, on one side of which was a piece of waste ground that was up for sale as a building site. Mr. Gamble had frequently speculated on its value and whether it would make a profitable investment. He could not make up his mind. It depended a great deal on whether certain proposals for the building of factories nearby would materialise or not.

It was raining more heavily now, and he turned up the collar of his overcoat. A nasty night, cold as well as wet. He would be glad for the warmth and comfort of his house.

Almost without knowing it, he quickened his pace. His glass of sherry would be very welcome. As he came near the waste ground, he heard the sound of footsteps behind him — quick, sharp footsteps — but he was not a curious man and he did not look round.

He was abreast of the waste ground now, and the footsteps were close behind him. They didn't seem to be as quick as they had been. He expected them to pass him.

But they didn't. They lingered behind him, adjusting their pace to his.

Mr. Gamble had now reached the shadow of the trees that grew in the waste ground, near the edge of the pavement. Their gaunt and spreading branches hung over him like a canopy, dripping water intermittently. There was little light here. The council had been sparing with the lamp standards.

And in the darkest patch under the trees, the footsteps caught up with him . . .

★　★　★

The dinner that Mr. Gamble had been looking forward to remained uneaten. The glass of sherry he would have sipped, before the fire in the lounge, remained in the bottle. Miss Emily Gamble, with a growing and not unnatural anxiety, waited for the arrival of her brother until nearly half-past eight. But he did not come.

By nine o'clock, she was trying to make up her mind what she ought to do. At half-past ten, she telephoned the police station.

Mr. Gamble was not found until just after dawn on the following morning. He was sprawled under a bush on the piece of waste ground. He was quite dead, and tightly tied about his thin neck was a length of the same type of red tape with which he had been accustomed to tie up the bundles of documents in his office.

2

Superintendent Robert Budd, that stout and lethargic man, was in a particularly irritable mood that morning. Everything had conspired to annoy him since he had got up.

To start with, in that aggravating way they sometimes have, the boiler had gone out during the night. In consequence, he had to put up with a tepid bath. On the top of this, his elderly housekeeper, a woman of whom Mr. Budd lived in constant dread, had frizzled his bacon, and he detested frizzled bacon. To put the final touch to this series of petty irritations, when it was time to leave his neat little villa in Streatham to go to Scotland Yard, his ancient car refused to start. He was forced to travel to Whitehall by bus.

As a result, by the time he reached his small and cheerless office, his temper was considerably ruffled. He wedged himself into his desk chair and fumbled in his waistcoat pocket for one of his evil-smelling black cigars. It was unusually early for him to smoke, but he felt in need of something to soothe his nerves.

When it was lit, he blew out a cloud of acrid smoke and turned his attention to the forms and reports that were awaiting him. There was nothing of particular interest — mostly routine matters concerned with the final clearing up of a rather dull case that he had recently completed.

He dealt with them as quickly as possible, tossed them into the outgoing basket, and settled back in his chair. There was no sign, as yet, of Sergeant Leek. That melancholy individual was probably wandering about somewhere, but he hadn't arrived in the office, a fact for which Mr. Budd was not a little thankful. He felt that Leek, on the top of all the other things he had had to put up with that morning, would be the last straw. All the same, the sergeant would have to be reprimanded for his lateness. It was getting too habitual.

It was nearly half an hour later before Leek put in an appearance. He drifted into the office, blinked sleepily at Mr. Budd, and said good morning.

'Do you know what the time is?' inquired the stout man.

Leek shook his head. 'Can't say I do. You see, me watch has gone wrong.'

'I shouldn't think it had ever been right. Aren't there any clocks where you live?'

'There's my alarm clock,' said the sergeant, taking off his shabby raincoat and hanging it on a peg behind the door. 'But there's somethin' the matter with it.'

'Gone rusty from lack of use, I expect,' broke in Mr. Budd sarcastically. 'You know, this'll have to stop.'

'I've just told you. It's already stopped.'

'I'm not talking about the clock,' snarled Mr. Budd. 'I mean this business of comin' into the office just when you think you will. You're s'pposed to be here at a certain hour, an' you never are. You're always late.'

'It's surprising isn't it?' remarked Leek. 'Do you know, when I was a little boy, I could never get anywhere on time.'

'You're not a little boy now. You're s'pposed to be a detective-sergeant in the C.I.D. — though how you ever became one is the biggest mystery I've ever had to deal with — '

'I got me promotion through diligence an' attention to me duty,' answered the sergeant proudly. 'That's what they said.'

'Who said?'

'The commissioners.'

'They must've been drunk. Maybe they muddled you up with somebody else. Let's see a bit o' this diligence an' attention to duty.'

'I do me best,' said the sergeant. 'I'm always ready when I'm wanted.'

'When you're here. Why were you late this mornin'?'

'I've been studyin'. Burnin' the midnight oil, as the sayin' goes.'

Mr. Budd eyed him through a cloud of smoke. 'Oh, you've been studyin', 'ave you?' he grunted. 'What's bitten you this time?'

'I've got a new 'obby.'

'Somnambulism?'

'No, that ain't what it's called. I don't know what somnam — whatever-you-call-it — means.'

'You surprise me,' said Mr. Budd. 'You've been practically doin' it all your life. Look it up in the dictionary.'

'This thing I've taken up's scientific. It's goin' to help me a lot in me career.'

'The only thing that's goin' to help you, is to get down to a bit of honest work. *That's* somethin' you haven't tried yet.'

The sergeant looked aggrieved. 'I don't know what you mean about that. Look at the hours an' hours I put in.'

'Sleepin'. Well, what is this wonderful new hobby you're messin' about with? If it's anythin' like your racin' an' your football pools . . . '

'This is serious. All that other stuff was frivolous. This is scientific.'

'So you said before. What are you up to? Tryin' to fill yourself with a little atomic energy?'

'I'll show yer,' said Leek. He came over to the stout superintendent's desk and, leaning slightly forward, fixed his rather watery eyes on Mr. Budd. The expression on his lean and melancholy face was so extraordinary that his superior could only stare at him in astonishment.

'Look at me,' said the sergeant in a deep, sepulchral tone. 'Look at me.'

'I'm lookin' at you. What the deuce is the matter with you?'

'You can't take your eyes off mine,' went on Leek. He raised a bony hand and began to pass it in front of the astonished Mr. Budd's face. 'You cannot move. You feel heavy.'

'Have you gone barmy at last? What the dickens do you think you're playin' at?'

Leek's face remained strained into an agonized expression of concentration. 'You cannot move,' he repeated in the same charnel-house tone. 'You wish to sleep . . . sleep . . . sleep.' The tips of his lean fingers almost tickled the end of Mr. Budd's nose. 'Sleep,' continued Leek with a diabolical glare. 'Relax an' sleep.'

'I don't want to sleep, confound you,' snapped Mr. Budd. 'D'you think everybody's like you? Stop this foolery.'

'You are sinkin' into oblivion,' said

Leek, ignoring the interruption, and continuing to glare fiendishly and wave his hands about. 'You feel yourself goin' down . . . down . . . down.'

'If you don't stop this tommyrot,' growled Mr. Budd, 'you'll not only feel yourself goin' down, you'll *be* down — in the nearest padded cell. What *is* all this tripe you're puttin' across, eh?'

'I'm hypnotisin' you,' explained Leek.

'You couldn't hypnotise a dead cat! So that's what you were up to, eh? I thought you'd gone stark raving mad.'

'Somethin' must've gone wrong,' said Leek with a puzzled frown. 'I can't understand it. I hypnotised meself in the mirror last night, an' put meself to sleep easily.'

'That doesn't surprise me. If you'd hypnotised yourself *awake*, now that would be somethin'. What d'you want to go messin' about with all this nonsense for?'

'Don't you see how useful it's goin' ter be?' asked Leek. 'Supposin' I get to grips with some desperate crook. All I've got to do is hypnotise 'im.'

'An' he'll either think you're a homicidal maniac, an' run like 'ell, or bash you, good an' proper while you're tryin' to put the 'fluence on him. Of all the fool things you've ever got into your head, this is about the craziest. If you start doin' to anybody else what you was tryin' to do to me, you'll land in the looney bin.'

The house telephone rang at that moment, and Mr. Budd broke off, stretched out his hand and picked up the receiver. 'Hello,' he called; and the voice of Colonel Blair, the assistant commissioner, came over the wire. 'Yes, sir, speakin'.' Mr. Budd listened for a moment. 'All right, sir, I'll come along at once.'

He put the receiver back on its rest, stubbed out the end of his cigar in the ashtray, and got heavily to his feet. 'It looks as though we was goin' to be busy,' he remarked. 'So you'd better get this hypnotism bug out of your system an' start puttin' your mind on the job you get paid for — though why they pay you anythin' at all is beyond me.' He lumbered out of the office before the melancholy Leek had time to reply.

Colonel Blair, neat and dapper as usual, was sitting behind his desk when Mr. Budd entered. There was a sheet of paper on the blotting-pad in front of him, and he held a pencil in his well-manicured fingers with which he had apparently been scrawling notes. 'Sit down, Superintendent,' he said, nodding towards a chair in front of the big desk. 'I've got a job for you. Rather a queer business.'

Mr. Budd lowered himself gingerly into the chair. It was a large chair, but his bulk filled it.

'The body of a man was found early this morning,' continued the assistant commissioner, picking up the sheet of paper and glancing at it as he spoke, 'lying under some bushes on a piece of waste ground at Wellington Park. The body was discovered by a workman who usually took a short cut across this waste ground, which is up for sale as a building site. This man, Grigg, reported the matter to the police, who eventually got in touch with us.'

'What time was the discovery made, sir?'

'Just before seven p.m. I know what you're thinking. The local people took a long time before reporting the matter to us, eh?'

Mr. Budd nodded. 'Wellington Park is in the metropolitan area.'

'Exactly,' agreed Colonel Blair. 'The matter should've been reported to the Yard at once. The superintendent at Wellington Park has already been reprimanded. However, to get back to this business. The dead man has been identified as a Mr. Humphrey Gamble, a solicitor who lived in Allardyce Road a short distance away from the place where his body was found. His sister, who keeps house for him, was expecting him home to dinner. When he failed to turn up, she notified the police.'

'Had she any reason to suppose that anythin' had happened to him?' asked Mr. Budd. 'I mean, sir, it's not unusual for a feller not to turn up for dinner.'

'You'll have to find out from the woman herself. I've only got the barest details here. There's no doubt that it's a question of murder. The man couldn't possibly have strangled himself.'

'Strangled, was he?' interpolated Mr. Budd, opening his half-closed eyes suddenly.

'Yes. And this is the queer thing about it. He was strangled with a piece of red tape — the kind that lawyers use for tying up documents.'

'His own?'

Colonel Blair shook his head. 'I can't tell you that. In fact, I've told you all I know. You'll have to find out the rest for yourself. I'm putting you in charge of the case. You'd better get along to Wellington Park as soon as you can.'

There was a note of dismissal in his voice, and Mr. Budd hauled himself out of the embrace of the chair with difficulty. 'I'll go along at once, sir.'

'You'll be taking Detective-Sergeant Leek with you.'

'Yes, sir,' said Mr. Budd a little wearily.

The suspicion of a twinkle showed in Colonel Blair's shrewd eyes. 'Well, good luck. It may turn out to be quite a simple

24

matter, or it may not. Whichever it is, I've every confidence in the way you'll handle it.'

'Thank you, sir,' murmured Mr. Budd, and he left the office.

A lawyer strangled with a piece of red tape? That was something a bit out of the rut, he thought as he made his way ponderously back to his own room. It *might* prove to be simple, but Mr. Budd had a hunch that it wouldn't.

And his hunches nearly always turned out to be right.

3

Superintendent Porterhouse, attached to the Wellington Park C.I.D., belied his name. There was nothing beefy about him. He was a short thin man with close-cropped dark hair and a sliver of moustache streaking the lower portion of his upper lip. His expression was slightly saturnine. Superintendent Porterhouse was not a popular man, either with his colleagues at the police station or his superiors. Mr. Budd took a dislike to him on sight, and he felt that the dislike was mutual.

It was a wet, unpleasant morning. The waste ground was muddy. The place where the dead body of Mr. Humphrey Gamble had been found was not very far from the road. Rank grass grew under a clump of evergreen bushes, and it was here that the body of Mr. Gamble had been dragged.

The body itself had been removed and

taken to the mortuary, but its position had been carefully marked, and the police photographs were fairly clear. Mr. Budd was able to get a pretty good idea of how everything had looked when the workman, Grigg, had made his gruesome discovery.

'He was attacked over there — on the pavement,' said Porterhouse, jerking his head towards a spot a few yards away from where they were standing. 'He was dragged to this place. You can see the double track of his heels in the mud and grass.'

'I've seen 'em,' grunted Mr. Budd.

'We've established the fact that he was killed about seven o'clock last evening,' went on Porterhouse a little triumphantly.

'How d'you make that out?'

'The ticket collector at the station. He knew Gamble well. He remembers him passing the barrier last night at five minutes to seven. Came on the six-fifty-three. It 'ud take him roughly about five minutes to walk from the station to this place.'

Mr. Budd could find no fault with this

conclusion. In spite of the fact that he didn't like Superintendent Porterhouse, he had to admit that there were no flies on him. He obviously knew his job.

Mr. Humphrey Gamble had been on his way home, then, when he had been attacked and strangled. The first thing, of course, was to seek for some kind of motive.

'Was he robbed?' he asked.

Porterhouse shook his head. 'No. That was the first thing that occurred to me, naturally. Nothing, so far as is known, was taken from his pockets. He was carrying a wallet with a considerable sum in notes, and a gold watch. They were still on the body when it was found.'

'Briefcase?'

'It's not known yet whether he was carrying one. The ticket collector can't remember. Of course, if he was, then that might have been the murderer's objective. No briefcase was found with the body.'

'Have you been in touch with the dead man's office?'

The superintendent nodded. 'Just notified them of the discovery. I expect you'll be interviewing them.'

'I shall. How did they take the news? Did they seem surprised?'

'Very. Apparently, Gamble was the only member of the firm; there isn't a partner. There's a kind of managing clerk. His name's Timothy Smithson. Been with the firm for donkey's years. It was him I spoke to. He couldn't believe it at first.'

'Who identified the body? The sister?'

'Yes. Miss Emily Gamble.'

'We'll go along and see her,' said Mr. Budd. He looked round at the rather depressing scene that had provided Mr. Humphrey Gamble with his last resting place. 'There's nothing much here. I suppose you searched pretty thoroughly?'

'Went all over the vicinity with a fine-toothed comb. Nothing at all, not even a cigarette end.'

'Come on, then. We'll see what the dead man's sister has to say.' He moved heavily off towards the waiting police car. Leek, who had been standing rather miserably, staring at nothing in particular, joined him as he picked his way over the muddy ground. Superintendent Porter-house had lingered behind to speak to one of his men, and Leek took advantage of this fact to make his suggestion.

'I say,' he said in a low voice, 'what about me trying a bit of hypnotism on this woman, eh? If I put 'er under the influence of me eye, she'd have to tell the truth.'

Mr. Budd gave him a withering glance. 'Now look here,' he said severely. 'If I catch you so much as blinkin' an optic at the woman, I'll have you up before the chief commissioner, so I'm warnin' you.'

The melancholy sergeant's lean face fell. 'I'm only tryin' ter be helpful. It 'ud save a lot o' time an' trouble.'

'I've never given you credit for much sense,' growled Mr. Budd, 'but I didn't think even you could be so dim-witted. Quite apart from the fact that you know no more about hypnotism than a fossilised rabbit, haven't you heard of the regulations? A witness has got to be interrogated in a certain manner.'

'This might be the beginnin' of a new method,' argued Leek, reluctant to be done out of his brilliant idea. 'I can see it revolutionising the whole of the police force.'

'So can I. An' the first person it 'ud revolutionise 'ud be you! Get all these silly ideas out of your head an' concentrate on doin' your job properly.'

Leek sighed. It was useless arguing with Mr. Budd. It seemed a pity, however, that he couldn't get a chance to prove the advantages of his suggestion. It was all very well to talk about regulations — he knew all about *them*. But it was time to instil fresh ideas. For a long time, the sergeant had been studying the subject, from various books acquired from his local library, and he reckoned he'd got it all at his fingertips. The fact that he had failed with Mr. Budd was just one of those things that happened sometimes. Maybe he'd been a bit nervous and hadn't concentrated enough.

It never entered his head that he was no good at it. Leek was always convinced that whatever went wrong with his schemes was through no fault of his. Look at the time he'd taken up football pools. He'd got an all-correct line almost the first time. The fact that he'd forgotten to post the coupon was just bad luck. And then there was racing. That had definitely been the fault of the horses.

Superintendent Porterhouse joined them and broke into the sergeant's thoughts. 'It isn't far to Gamble's house,' he said. 'Just up the road and round the corner. Hardly worth taking the car.'

Mr. Budd grunted. He detested walking, even a few yards, if he could avoid it. Firmly he walked to the police car, opened the door, and squeezed himself in beside the driver. With a scarcely perceptible shrug of his shoulders, Porterhouse got in the back with Leek.

Allardyce Road was like hundreds of other roads all over the country. It was trim and neat and very new. There was a strip of grass running between the edge of the kerb and the pavement, planted with small and rather wilting trees, each tied to a wooden support.

It was an extraordinary sidelight on the mentality of councils and corporations that wherever they found trees growing in luxurious maturity, they immediately cut them down. Yet they would spend a great deal of time, money and labour planting these anaemic specimens, which would take many years to become fully grown, and would then no doubt be cut down in their turn by future councils and corporations if, in the meanwhile, all living things, including trees and councils and corporations, were not destroyed by the atomic bomb.

This passionate desire for destruction seemed to have become so firmly implanted in the human race, even in small things, Mr. Budd mused to himself, that unless it was checked, and a saner and more mature outlook took its place, it would eventually destroy the world. What was the use of this so-called progress if it took from people the peace and beauty of their natural heritage?

Let them return to the simpler things so abundantly provided for them; things that all the councils and corporations, the scientists and the manufacturers, banded together in a body, could not give them:

the hushed beauty of dawn; the peaceful loveliness of a summer evening; the scent of freshly cut grass; the smell of autumn and the fairyland of ice and snow in winter; the sea breaking gently on the beach, or dashing stormily against the rocks; the drowsy hum of bees on a hot summer afternoon. These things could be created by increasing the rates, or tinkering about with apparatus in a laboratory.

But they could be destroyed. It rested with humanity to decide. Let people rise up in anger against the councils and the corporations who, for the sake of greed, were ruining the countryside. Let them rise up in anger, too, against the scientists and the manufacturers who, in the name of progress, were filling the skies with noise, and the roads and byways with hurtling juggernauts in an incessant, mad race for more and more speed; who were flinging monstrous contrivances into space to compete with the universe, so that even the tranquil beauty of a moonlit night might soon be denied. Let them rise up against these things — before it was too late.

So ran Mr. Budd's thoughts as the police car came to a halt opposite a small, neat house on the left of Allardyce Road. The oblong front garden consisted of a lawn and several flowerbeds containing the remains of rose bushes which, the expert eye of the superintendent saw, had been sadly neglected. Mr. Budd's hobby was the growing of roses. The garden of his little house at Streatham contained a variety of these lovely flowers, and such spare time as he had at his disposal was spent in carefully tending them.

The inside of the house where the dead man had lived was as neat as the exterior. The furniture was old and of a period when craftsmen took a pride in their workmanship. Everything was polished carefully; and, Mr. Budd thought, it would have been difficult to find even a speck of dust anywhere.

Miss Emily Gamble, her thin face betraying her recent grief, ushered them into the lounge. She was an angular woman without any pretentions to beauty. Her greying hair was neatly combed tightly across her narrow head, and dressed into a bun on the nape of her rather scraggy neck. She was dressed in an old and rather shabby black dress that enhanced the sallowness of her complexion and the swollen redness of her eyes.

Mr. Budd murmured a few conventional words of sympathy and apologised for having to intrude at such a time.

'Please, don't worry about that,' said Miss Gamble. 'I quite understand. I'm ready to do anything I can to help you.' She twisted a wispy handkerchief in her bony hands and looked at them rather pathetically. 'It was a terrible shock to me, as you can imagine. I can't seem to realise that it can really be true. Why should anyone want to kill Humphrey?'

'You don't know of anybody who bore Mr. Gamble a grudge?' inquired Mr. Budd.

'Oh, no. I'm quite sure there wasn't anybody. My brother lived very quietly, you know. Most of his time was spent at his office.'

'Who were his personal friends?'

'He didn't have many. You see, we haven't lived here very long,' she added almost apologetically. 'Only just over nine months.'

'But you had friends out of this district? Where did you live before you came here?'

'We had a flat in Putney. Humphrey didn't make a lot of friends. We knew one or two people, of course. But you could hardly call them friends; just acquaintances. You see, my brother liked to spend his evenings quietly. He never encouraged visitors.'

Mr. Budd tried to evolve a picture of the dead man in his mind's eye. He would rise, probably early. Bath, shave, and come down to breakfast. Catch his train to town, spend the day at his office, return home in the evening, have his dinner, read the paper or perhaps a book, and retire fairly early to bed. The same routine, day in, day out, for weeks, months, years. Nothing much in that kind of life to provide a motive for murder.

'Did Mr. Gamble ever stay late in

town?' he asked. 'Did he belong to any club?'

Miss Gamble shook her head. 'No. He was always glad to get home as quickly as he could after the day's business.'

'He never stayed away for any length of time? A few days, or a weekend perhaps?'

'No. It was with the greatest difficulty that I used to persuade him to go for a short summer holiday.'

'And on the occasions that you did, I suppose you went with him?'

'Oh, yes. He would never have gone alone.'

Mr. Budd stifled a yawn. If ever there was a man whose life seemed to preclude any possible motive for murder, it was Mr. Humphrey Gamble. And yet someone *had* killed him; had slipped that length of red tape round his wizened neck and drawn it tight. Somewhere in Mr. Gamble's apparently blameless life, there must exist a clue to this motive, unless he had been the victim of a homicidal maniac.

But there was the question of the method of murder here. Surely the coincidence of a homicidal maniac, selecting his victim haphazardly, and armed with a length of legal red tape, choosing a *solicitor* by chance, was a little too much to even consider. It was far more likely that the victim had been chosen *because* of his profession. The murder weapon and that profession fitted so perfectly.

'Have you noticed any change in your brother lately, miss?' asked Mr. Budd after a short pause. 'Did he appear worried or upset durin' the past few weeks?'

She smiled a little wanly. 'It would have taken a great deal to upset my brother. He was very unemotional and even-tempered. I don't think I can remember when I've seen him upset.'

'Not even when he was worried about some client or legal business?'

'He never discussed his business with me. It was mostly concerned with property, you know. He never undertook any other business.'

'And so far as you know, he hadn't any close friends?'

'Well, there was Mr. Grindthorpe. I don't know whether you could call him a *close* friend. He's a solicitor, and my brother used to lunch with him quite frequently.'

Mr. Budd made a note of Mr. Grindthorpe, and his address. He would have to be seen, in case he might know anything that would give a hint to the identity of the murderer.

He put several further questions to Miss Gamble, mostly slight variations on his previous ones, but he gathered nothing that was in the least helpful.

A search of the dead man's effects produced nothing of any importance. He had obviously been very methodical and neat. Such documents as there were, were tied up and docketed. It struck Mr. Budd as ironical that they were tied up with red tape, but it was something only to be expected from a man in Mr. Gamble's profession. They consisted almost entirely of receipted bills, cancelled cheques, and household accounts. There was a file containing pass sheets from the dead man's bank that showed him to have had a considerable credit balance. And that was all. Nothing to suggest why he had died so suddenly and so tragically. Nothing to suggest a clue to the person who had killed him.

Perhaps the office would yield better results. Mr. Budd decided to pay a visit there without further delay.

*   *   *

The person sitting in a corner of the little teashop took a sip of coffee from the cup on the table and consulted a small notebook with interest.

On the page it was open to was a list of names. It wasn't a very long list, but it occupied the owner of the book for some time. A smile, and not a particularly pleasant one, twisted the face bent so intently over the notebook. The hand, holding a cheap ballpoint pen, hovered for a moment over the name at the head of the list.

Presently the pen drew a red line through the name of Humphrey Gamble.

4

Miss Catkin was in a state of fluttering excitement. During the whole of her long employment with the firm of Gamble, Chalkit, Gamble and Gamble, she had never experienced anything like this. She had frequently read in the newspapers of murders and robberies and other horrible happenings; but she had treated them more or less perfunctorily, being more interested in the latest society scandal or the frequent divorces of her favourite film star. It had never even remotely occurred to her that she, Sophia Catkin, would, or could, be mixed up in such a thing.

And here she was — right in the middle of a murder! The mere thought of it sent a thrill through her meagre body. And she was astonished, and a little dismayed, to find that the thrill was not unpleasant.

The first intimation she had received of the murder had come to her from Timothy Smithson. They had both been rather surprised when Mr. Gamble had failed to put in an appearance at his usual time. Such a thing had only happened once before, and on that occasion it had been due to the fact that he had been suffering from a severe chill. Otherwise, punctuality and Mr. Gamble were synonymous.

She had been in the middle of typing out a long and rather intricate lease when Timothy Smithson had brought her the news. She had seen by the expression on his face as he approached her that something serious had happened.

'It's . . . it's Mr. Humphrey,' said the managing clerk in answer to her inquiry. 'It's Mr. Humphrey.'

'What's the matter with Mr. Humphrey?' she asked.

'He's dead.' Timothy Smithson stammered slightly and seemed a trifle dazed. 'The police h-have just r-rung up.'

'The police!' exclaimed Miss Catkin shrilly. 'Why the police?'

'It was murder,' broke in Smithson. 'He was murdered last night.'

'I don't believe it!' declared Miss

Catkin. 'There must be some mistake.'

Timothy Smithson shook his head. He pulled out a handkerchief from his pocket and wiped the palms of his hands.

'No, no,' he said tremulously. 'There's no mistake. He was strangled with a piece of red tape.'

'A piece of red tape,' repeated Miss Catkin. She looked at the piles of neatly tied documents stacked everywhere around her. 'Do you mean — like that?'

'I suppose so,' said Smithson. 'That's what they said. They'll be coming here soon.'

'Where?' said Miss Catkin in a hushed voice. 'Where did it happen?'

Timothy Smithson moistened his lips before he replied. 'Near his home. He was found on a piece of waste ground near his home. They didn't tell me much.' He looked rather helplessly round the dingy office. 'I wonder what we ought to do,' he added.

'We can't do anything except wait for the police,' answered Miss Catkin practically. 'I *still* can't believe it. Why should anyone want to murder Mr. Humphrey?'

The old man shook his head. 'I don't know, but it must be true. It was the superintendent at Wellington Park police station who rang up. They couldn't have made any mistake.'

Miss Catkin got up from her typewriter. She went quickly over to the door of the private office — the office where Mr. Gamble would never sit behind his littered writing-table again.

'What are you going to do?' asked the chief clerk.

'I'm going to look up his engagements for today,' said Miss Catkin briskly. 'We must try and keep things going on as usual. If there are any appointments with clients, *you* must see them. You're just as capable of dealing with most of the business as Mr. Gamble is — was,' she corrected hastily. 'We'd best not say anything about this dreadful murder to anyone until after the police have been. I'm sure that's what they would prefer. If there's anything you can't deal with, just say that Mr. Gamble's not in today.'

She opened the door and disappeared into the inner office. It was remarkable how she had suddenly taken charge. Old Timothy Smithson stood looking after her, gently rubbing his forehead.

It looked even dingier than usual inside Mr. Gamble's office. The rain was beating on the window, with its wire blind that shut out such a great deal of light. The dust lay thickly on the bundles of documents that flanked the blotting-pad on the writing-table. It wouldn't be long, thought Miss Catkin with a little shiver, before Mr. Gamble would be dust, too.

It seemed impossible to believe that he would never again occupy the shabby chair in which she had so often seen him. She remembered the last occasion when she had — the previous afternoon when she had been worrying over being late with the tea. How futile that seemed now.

She went over to the writing-table and opened the engagement book. The page for that day bore scarcely any entries in Mr. Gamble's small neat writing. There was nothing for the morning. In the afternoon, at three-thirty, there was a note concerning the lease she had been typing out that morning. The owner of the property to which it referred was coming in to see Mr. Gamble.

There was nothing of any importance. Miss Catkin shut the book and paused for a few moments before going back to the outer office. She wondered what would happen to the firm. She supposed that Mr. Gamble had made a will, but who would benefit? Was there anyone apart from Miss Emily Gamble in the family? Perhaps old Timothy Smithson would know. Mr. Gamble had never mentioned any relations, but then he had never spoken much about himself at all. He had been a very self-contained man, austere and cold.

She turned her eyes towards the old-fashioned safe in the corner. Mr. Gamble carried the keys with him. Probably the police had them.

Miss Catkin returned to the outer office. 'There are no appointments for this morning, Mr. Smithson,' she announced. 'Mr. Bryant is coming this afternoon at three-thirty about his lease. You'll be able to deal with him, won't you?' The managing clerk nodded slowly. 'By that time, we shall have seen the police, I expect. Then we'll know more about it. What do you think will happen to the firm?'

Timothy Smithson considered before he replied. 'I really don't know,' he answered at last. 'Of course, Miss Emily is the next of kin.'

'She couldn't run the business.'

'No, no, but she could either sell it, or put in a qualified lawyer to run it for her.'

'You're fully qualified, aren't you?'

'Yes.'

'Perhaps you'll be asked to carry on the business,' suggested Miss Catkin hopefully.

Old Smithson took off his spectacles and wiped them carefully with the silk handkerchief from his breast pocket. 'I should like that. Do you know, Miss Catkin, it's always been my ambition to have my own practice.' He shook his head. 'I never had enough money.'

'Well, you never know your luck. I'm going to make some tea.'

The managing clerk looked shocked. 'We have never had tea at this time in the morning.'

'We're going to have it this morning,' declared Miss Catkin firmly, and she went off to the dark little cubicle containing the stove.

Timothy Smithson replaced his spectacles and sat down at his usual table. But for once he didn't work. Clasping his hands together, he rested his elbows on the table and let his chin sink until it was supported by his interlocked fingers. His eyes, behind the glasses, stared into vacancy. What a lot could happen in a short time, he thought, what a lot.

Miss Catkin brought him a cup of tea, and carried her own over to her typing table. Sitting down, she continued with the typing of the lease, which had been interrupted by the news of Mr. Gamble's death. It had to be finished before Mr. Bryant called to keep his three-thirty appointment.

★ ★ ★

Mr. Budd broke his journey to London at the mortuary to inspect the body of the dead man. The contents of the pockets had been laid out neatly, and these he examined with interest.

They consisted of a handsome gold watch, a worn leather wallet with the initials 'H.G.' in gold in one corner, a bunch of keys, a small quantity of loose change, a season ticket-holder with a season ticket — recently renewed — between Waterloo and Wellington Park, and a small packet bearing the name of a well-known jeweller.

'What's this?' inquired Mr. Budd, peering at it through half-closed eyes.

Porterhouse shook his head. 'We didn't open it. It was found in his overcoat pocket.'

'We'll open it now,' said Mr. Budd, and he proceeded to do so. Inside, resting on a bed of cotton wool, was a gold brooch. In small pearls it bore the interwoven initials E.G. 'Emily Gamble. It looks as if 'e was bringin' her a present.'

'Those might not be her initials,' remarked Superintendent Porterhouse.

'They might not be, but I should think it's most likely that they are. What's in the wallet?'

There was nothing very much. Seven pounds in notes, a receipted bill for the brooch, a ticket for some cleaning, and a slip of paper on which had been scrawled the figures 7628. That was all.

'That could be a telephone number,' said Porterhouse.

'It could be,' agreed Mr. Budd, 'an', then again, it could be somethin' else. Hm. There's nothin' much here to help us. You say there was no sign of a briefcase?'

'We didn't find one.'

'It may have been what the murderer was after. We can rule out ordinary robbery, anyhow.' He yawned. 'You'd better have these things parcelled up an' sent to the Yard. I'd like a copy of the post-mortem report, too. I'll drop you at the police station.'

On the way back to London, Mr. Budd huddled himself in his big overcoat, clasped his hands over his capacious stomach, and closed his eyes.

Sergeant Leek, in the opposite corner of the seat, his long, thin face looking more miserable than usual, stared out at the wet pavements and the falling rain. He felt discontented and frustrated. He was quite certain that, given the chance, he could have extracted a great deal more out of the dead man's sister by hypnotism than his superior had by his questions. Hypnotism released the inhibitions of the subconscious — at least that was what it said in the book he had been studying. Things that people didn't even know about. Maybe this woman knew something, deep down, that'd give them a clue to the murder.

'What's on your mind?' inquired the voice of Mr. Budd from the depths of his overcoat collar. 'Plannin' to hypnotise the chief commissioner inter makin' you a chief constable, I suppose?'

'It ain't a thing to joke about,' said Leek. 'You'd be surprised what 'ypnotism can do.'

'I wouldn't. I'd only be surprised if you could do anythin' with it. I've been thinkin' over this business of Gamble. It's queer, you know — it's very queer. There's a nasty sense of humour on the murderer's part in usin' red tape. It's like killin' a butcher with a poleaxe. Red tape, you might say, is one o' the tools of a lawyer's trade.'

'D'you mean that Gamble was killed by a lawyer?'

'That wasn't what I was gettin' at, but it's an idea.'

'I get 'em now and again,' remarked the gratified Leek.

'You've got to do somethin' to earn your salary, even if it's only once in a blue moon. But there might well be somethin' in that idea o' yours. We've got a lawyer mixed up in this business, apart from the victim. Mr. Grindthorpe, who the dead man used to lunch with quite frequently. Hm. I wonder what sort of a feller *he* is.'

'He lives at Putney.'

'I know,' said Mr. Budd a little irritably. 'We got his address from Miss Gamble. You don't have to tell me somethin' I know already. Yes, he lives at Putney,' he added thoughtfully. 'An' that's where the Gambles lived before they moved to Allardyce Road. Maybe this feller Grindthorpe 'ull be well worth a visit.'

He closed his eyes again and relapsed

into silence. He didn't speak again until the car drew up outside the offices of Gamble, Chalkit, Gamble and Gamble.

'Here we are,' he said unnecessarily, and hoisted himself out of the car.

Miss Catkin received him in the outer office with ill-concealed excitement. She had been waiting all the morning for this moment. Old Timothy Smithson showed no signs of excitement. They might have been clients instead of representatives of the C.I.D.

'I'm afraid this is an unpleasant business,' said Mr. Budd after he had introduced himself and the sergeant. 'The news must have been a shock to you.'

'Oh, indeed it was,' said Miss Catkin, clasping her hands. 'Isn't it dreadful? Poor Mr. Gamble! Who would have thought such a thing could happen to *him*?'

'You know of no possible motive that might have led someone to murder him?' asked Mr. Budd.

'No, I'm sure there was nothing.'

'There must've been somethin', you know. Has there been any trouble? I mean, could some client, who Mr. Gamble prosecuted or defended, have got it into his head that he had a grievance?'

'We never went in for that kind of business,' put in Timothy Smithson, shaking his head. 'At least, not in Mr. Humphrey's time. I can't remember when we took a case to court. Mr. Humphrey hated litigation.'

'Well, that's somethin' new on me,' said Mr. Budd. 'A lawyer who hated litigation! It don't seem possible.'

'It's true in Mr. Gamble's case,' said Miss Catkin. 'He refused all cases which might come to the courts. He used to recommend anyone who came here with that kind of case to go to Mr. Grindthorpe.'

'Ah, yes, I've heard of him,' murmured Mr. Budd. 'Lives at Putney, doesn't he?'

'That's right,' agreed Miss Catkin. 'But his offices are just round the corner.'

'Hm,' said Mr. Budd. 'Now, perhaps you can tell me if you've noticed any change in Mr. Gamble recently. Has he been moody, depressed — anything that was different to his usual demeanour?'

'I didn't notice any difference in him at all,' said the managing clerk. 'Mind you, if there had been anything bothering him, Mr. Humphrey wouldn't have shown it.'

This bore out what Miss Emily Gamble had said, thought the stout man.

'He did something he hadn't done for months,' said Miss Catkin. 'He left a quarter of an hour earlier yesterday afternoon.'

'Oh, he did, did 'e?' said Mr. Budd. 'Do you know why he did that?'

'Mr. Humphrey never accounted for what he did,' said Timothy Smithson. 'Unless, of course, it was necessary in the course of business.'

'Then this couldn't have had anything to do with business?'

'Yes, it could,' answered the managing clerk. 'It was only when it was necessary that either Miss Catkin or I should know about it that he told us.'

'I see,' said Mr. Budd. A reticent man, Mr. Humphrey Gamble. A man who didn't believe in taking anybody into his confidence unless he had to. With such a man, there might have been anything in his life that could have led to murder. 'When the body was found,' he went on, and Miss Catkin gave a little shiver, 'there was a packet in the overcoat pocket from a firm of jewellers. Do you know anything about that?'

They both shook their heads.

'It contained,' said Mr. Budd, 'a gold brooch with the initials E.G. in small pearls.'

'Those would be Miss Gamble's initials,' broke in Miss Catkin quickly. 'She's — was — is.' She broke off in confusion.

'She's still his sister,' said Mr. Budd. 'Do you know why he should've been taking her a present?'

'Maybe it was her birthday,' suggested Miss Catkin. 'Why don't you ask her?' she added sensibly.

'I intend to,' said Mr. Budd. 'When I was questionin' her, I hadn't seen this brooch. You're quite sure there's nothin' either of you can tell me that might help to throw some light on this business?'

There was nothing. They were both equally certain about this.

Mr. Budd sighed. It was going to be a difficult job. There was, up to the present, nothing to go on. Of course, it was early days yet, but it was Mr. Budd's experience that if a case was going to turn out to be an easy one, it was in the early days that it did so.

'I'd like to have a look at the dead man's office,' he said. 'There was a bunch of keys on the body' — Miss Catkin shivered again — 'an' among them there looks to be a safe key. Is there a safe in the office?'

Miss Catkin nodded. She was going to take Mr. Budd into the inner room, but it was Timothy Smithson who quietly interposed, to Miss Catkin's extreme disappointment.

The first thing that Mr. Budd spotted, as he looked round the drab office, was a pigskin briefcase. It stood on a chair near the writing table. 'Did that belong to Mr. Gamble?' he asked, pointing to it.

The managing clerk nodded.

'Did he usually leave it in the office, or take it home with him?' asked Mr. Budd.

'He only took it when he had some

papers he wanted to peruse at home,' answered Timothy Smithson. 'That wasn't very often.'

The superintendent went over and picked up the briefcase. It was locked. A search of the bunch of keys, however, soon discovered the key that belonged to it. Mr. Budd, under the rather disapproving eye of the old man, opened the briefcase.

There was very little inside. A few catalogues of auction sales, a list of properties for sale from an estate agent's, an architect's drawings of a bungalow. That was all. Well, it wasn't for the briefcase that Humphrey Gamble had been murdered. He very seldom carried it, apparently, so even if there *had* been anything in it that the murderer wanted, he couldn't have been sure that the dead man would have it with him. In fact, the odds were that he wouldn't.

Of course, there might be something else — something in Humphrey Gamble's pockets — that the murderer had taken. There was no means of telling what else he had had on him, apart from the things they had found. That was definitely the first thing to establish — a motive. And it didn't look as if it was going to be easy.

Mr. Budd put down the briefcase and turned his attention to the rest of the office. He went through it methodically, with the assistance of Leek, carefully examining the contents of the drawers in the writing-table, and the old fashioned filing-cabinets and cupboards. And he found nothing. Not the vestige of anything that could even remotely have a bearing on the solicitor's death. Miss Catkin, determined not to be done out of her excitement, brought in cups of tea, and remained to watch the proceedings. At last, there only remained the safe.

It was a very old safe. At one time it had been painted green, but age and dust had reduced the original colour to a nondescript hue that was neither green nor grey, but a combination of both.

Selecting the key from the bunch, Mr. Budd stooped with difficulty and inserted it in the lock. The door opened easily. The safe was divided into two compartments, an upper one for books and bulky documents, and a lower one that consisted of two drawers side by side.

The big man examined the contents of the top compartment first. There were a set of account books, and petty-cash book, a stamp book, and a number of leases. Of personal documents there was none.

He unlocked the drawers. One contained a small sum in notes and cash, amounting to thirty-seven pounds, some insurance stamps, and three insurance cards — Mr. Gamble's own, Miss Catkin's, and Smithson's. There was also a cheque book. That was all in that drawer. The other contained even less. Only a single long envelope with the superscription 'My Will' in neat and careful writing.

The envelope was unsealed, and Mr. Budd, after a moment of hesitation, drew out a double-folded sheet of foolscap.

Miss Catkin, her curiosity getting the better of her, came over close beside him and tried to peer over his arm. But Mr. Budd shifted the document so that she was unable to gain any information.

Timothy Smithson appeared to lack any interest in it at all. He stood in the middle of the room, his fingers gently pulling at his lower lip, and frowned at the empty chair behind the writing table.

And yet he *should* be interested, thought Mr. Budd, folding the will after a brief glance at the contents, and putting it back into its envelope. He should be very interested indeed.

For, after providing an annuity for his sister, Mr. Humphrey Gamble had left everything he possessed to his managing clerk.

5

Mr. Joseph Grindthorpe was totally unlike the preconceived notion that Mr. Budd had formed of him. From his name, he had expected to find a thin and cadaverous man, curt, and inclined to be rather irritable; whereas in actual fact, Mr. Grindthorpe was a stout and jovial little man with twinkling blue eyes, a double chin and a head that, if not completely bald, could not muster sufficient hair to do more than partially veil its nakedness.

The name 'Grindthorpe' would have suited Porterhouse, thought Mr. Budd, and 'Porterhouse' would have suited Grindthorpe. There was not much in a name, after all.

Mr. Grindthorpe's office was a great deal more modern than Mr. Gamble's. It was also a great deal less dusty. Mr. Grindthorpe's secretary was a young woman. Mr. Grindthorpe's managing clerk was an alert man of not more than forty, a distinct difference to old Timothy Smithson. And Mr. Grindthorpe was prepared to deal with any legal business that was likely to bring grist to his mill.

'This is really terrible news, terrible,' he said when the superintendent had explained the reason for his visit. 'I can't understand why anyone should want to kill old Gamble. I've known him for several years — and his sister. Lived close to me in Putney. Funny old chap, Humphrey. Didn't get much amusement out of life. Rather a stick in the mud. Lived to a timetable, everything done at the same hour every day. You know the type? Wouldn't suit me. I like a bit of gaiety after the day's work, eh? Still, we used to hit it off quite well together. Attraction of opposites, eh? There's a lot in that, you know.'

'I expect there is, sir,' said Mr. Budd.

'Oh, undoubtedly,' said Mr. Grind-thorpe, getting his second wind as it were, and starting again. 'Poor Gamble never had any life at all, in my opinion. Didn't play golf, didn't belong to any club, wasn't interested in women. Train in the morning to the office, train in the evening back home, glass of sherry before dinner, dinner, bed. Start the whole round all over again. What sort of life is that, eh?' Mr. Grindthorpe's round face expanded into a wide grin. 'Look at me,' he went on before Mr. Budd could get in a word. 'I work hard, but I play hard. Theatres, nightclubs, a round or so of golf at the weekend. No good working all the time. Not healthy for any man, eh?'

'I'd be glad,' said Mr. Budd firmly, as the other paused for breath, 'if you'd answer one or two questions.'

'Will if I can. Always willing to help, you know. Both on the side of the law, eh? Between you and me, Dickens was right.'

'When did you last see Mr. Gamble, sir?' interposed Mr. Budd, stemming the torrent of words that seemed to flow inexhaustibly from the little lawyer's mouth.

'Ah. Now when *did* I last see Gamble?' said Mr. Grindthorpe, pursing his cherubic lips. 'We lunched together . . . was it on the Wednesday, or the Thursday?'

'I'm askin' you that, sir,' said Mr. Budd patiently.

'Yes, yes, of course, of course. I'm just trying to remember. Ah, yes, it *was* the Wednesday.' Mr. Grindthorpe nodded his shining head. 'We discussed the rent act.'

'Mr. Gamble was just as usual?' asked Mr. Budd. 'He didn't seem to have anything on his mind?'

'Only the rent act,' chuckled the little lawyer. 'Dear me, we had a grand argument.'

'I'm sure you did, sir,' agreed Mr. Budd, stifling his exasperation with a supreme effort. 'I'm afraid I'm not interested in the rent act at the moment.'

'No, naturally,' said Mr. Grindthorpe. 'You want to know whether Gamble was his normal self, eh? Exactly. Well, he was. There was no difference in him at all.'

Mr. Budd sighed wearily. The same answer from everybody. Was there *nothing* that he could get his teeth into? Some sort of jumping-off point? He tried a new tack. 'I understand, sir,' he said, after a pause, 'that Mr. Gamble used to pass on a number of clients to you?'

'That's quite true. Gamble was only interested in property, you know. He wouldn't touch ordinary legal business. I daresay they told you that at his office, eh? He used to shove all those kinds of clients on to me.'

'There wasn't any trouble with any of them?'

'Well, there was one fellow who was rather annoyed. I soon soothed him down.'

'Why was he annoyed?'

'He thought Gamble had been rude to him,' said Mr. Grindthorpe with a chuckle. 'Probably right, too. Gamble had a habit, you know, of listening to what these people had to tell him before turning 'em down and sending 'em on to me. It riled some of them, particularly this chap I'm talking about. Apparently he told Gamble that he might have saved him the trouble of going into all the details of his case, if he'd no intention of acting for him. Gamble retorted that he hadn't got a case, anyway. He hadn't, either! You won't find anything there, you know. Not a motive for murder, eh?'

Mr. Budd agreed with him. He took the man's name and address, however, as a matter of precaution. You never could tell. There might be more in it than Mr. Grindthorpe knew.

'What was the case this feller wanted Mr. Gamble to handle for him?' he inquired.

'Question of annoyance from his neighbour,' said Mr. Grindthorpe. 'Silly. The neighbour's wife used to stand at the window and make faces at him whenever he came in or went out. That's all. I told him the same as Gamble had.' His face suddenly grew serious. 'I don't think you'll find a reasonable motive,' he said gravely. 'Poor Gamble was just the victim of some lunatic's lust to kill. It happened to be him, but it might have been anyone. The red tape's just a coincidence.'

'A very queer coincidence, sir,' remarked the superintendent.

Mr. Grindthorpe shrugged his shoulders. 'Possibly, possibly,' he answered. 'But these things happen, you know.'

There was obviously nothing more to be learned from Mr. Grindthorpe, and

Mr. Budd took his departure.

'What do we do now?' asked the sergeant hopefully.

'If you think we're goin' back to the Yard so that you can have a nap in the office, you can 'ave another think,' he grunted. 'We're goin' to see Gamble's bank manager.'

'What good's that goin' to do?'

'I don't know, but we've got to try everything.'

The bank was closed to the public when they got there, but Mr. Budd produced his credentials, and they were admitted to the manager's office.

He was a pleasant-faced man, and he was enjoying a cup of tea and a biscuit when they were shown in. 'Not often we have a visit from the police,' he said. 'What's the trouble? Nothing to do with the bank, or any of my staff, I hope?'

Mr. Budd told him the reason for their visit, and he listened gravely. 'Dear me, this is very sad,' he commented when Mr. Budd had finished. 'Humphrey Gamble was the last man I should have expected such a thing to happen to. Strangled with a piece of red tape . . . dreadful! Really, you know, it's shocking the amount of violence there is in the world these days.'

Mr. Budd agreed, and asked him about Mr. Gamble's accounts.

'He had two,' replied the bank manager. 'A private account and a business account. Both are in perfect order. He was a very meticulous man. Without being wealthy, he was quite comfortably off. The business was a prosperous one. He never indulged in anything that was in the least speculative. All his property deals were sound investments, either when he acted on his own behalf, or on behalf of his clients.'

'He hadn't drawn any unusual cheques lately?'

The bank manager shook his head. 'No. There has been nothing of the kind. He seldom exceeded the weekly amount he drew on his private account. It was a comparatively small amount. He paid most of his bills monthly, and by cheque.'

'What was his credit balance at the time of his death? Both on his private account and the business one.'

The bank manager mentioned sums that were considerable. 'I suppose it will all go to his sister,' he said, trying to acquire some information in his turn. 'Unless, he made a will.'

'I expect he did, sir,' said Mr. Budd cautiously. He wasn't there to give information, but to obtain it. 'There's nothin' at all, then, that you can tell me that might give us a line on the motive, sir?'

'No, I'm afraid I can't help you,' said the bank manager a little regretfully.

Mr. Budd felt that he would have been pleased to have been able to make some dramatic contribution to the inquiry into Mr. Humphrey Gamble's death. Thanking the manager for his trouble, and apologising for disturbing him, he left him and went back to the waiting police car.

'An' that's that,' remarked Leek pessimistically. 'Waste o' time, I call it.'

Mr. Budd made no comment. For once, he had to agree with that melancholy man.

'Where do we go from 'ere?' asked Leek.

'Back to the Yard.'

A beatific expression of satisfaction spread over the sergeant's face as he settled back in his seat. It had been a long day. Now, he saw the prospect of a little rest.

* * *

The meeting of the borough council in the Town Hall was over. Many things had been discussed, but few had reached the final stages of adoption. There had been a great deal of opposition to many of the proposals on the agenda.

For instance, the repainting of the light-standards. This had been the subject for argument at previous meetings. There were those in favour, and those who thought the painting could well be postponed for another year. Then there was the question of certain roads. The surfaces of these had, for a long time, been in a bad condition. While the necessity for repairs was admitted, there was a great deal of controversy concerning *which* roads should be included. The raising of the rents for certain council houses and flats also resulted in a division of opinions.

But the main bone of contention was the proposal to acquire, by compulsory purchase, a group of three cottages on the site of which the council wanted to erect a block of flats. The cottages were all inhabited by their respective owners. These people had occupied them for a considerable period; had spent a great deal of money in modernising them and on the gardens surrounding them. They were, not unnaturally, extremely annoyed at the prospect of having their homes taken away from them. The price that the council was prepared to pay them was grossly inadequate. But under the law, this legal robbery was permissible.

It was not the question of whether or not they could legally acquire the group of cottages for the pittance they were prepared to pay, or even the moral aspect, that bothered the borough council, of which Mr. Gilmore was such a shining light. It was the much more important consideration of public opinion. Just over a year ago there had been a considerable outcry in the press concerning the tragic result of one of their compulsory acquisitions. A new road had to be built and, unfortunately, a bungalow stood in the way of this venture. It had been built by a young man named Penfold, who had sunk all his savings, and his war gratuity, into it. That he was rather a neurotic type, due to a large extent to his war experiences, did not mitigate the council's moral responsibility for what happened.

For Richard Penfold, having fought the legal seizure of his home with every means in his power, and finding that he could do nothing to stop it, went quietly out into his little garden and shot himself.

There was a tremendous repercussion throughout the country. In the inquiry that followed Penfold's death, it was disclosed that the council had offered him two hundred and fifty pounds for land and property that had cost him over three thousand. The matter was brought up in the House of Commons, and Parliament gave power to local authorities to pay more in the future. But there was no rescinding of the law of compulsory purchase.

Penfold had taken a very drastic and possibly foolish way out of his difficulties. But who could tell how strong were the emotions of bitterness and despair that had driven him to do so?

It was the recollection of this unpleasant episode that caused a diversion of opinion regarding the cottages. It was unlikely that such a thing would happen again, but . . . ?

'We must act very carefully in this matter,' said Councillor Wishford. 'Isn't there, for instance, an alternative site?'

Councillor Cranbourne shook his head impatiently. He was one of the largest estate agents in the district, and had a personal interest in the proposed block of flats. Indeed, he was the instigator of the scheme. 'There's no other site so suitable,' he said. 'The cottages will have to go. We can offer 'em a fair price — nothing outrageous, of course. Our valuer will advise us there.'

The valuer was also Councillor Cranbourne's son-in-law, so there was no doubt that his advice would be reasonable. Eventually, the matter of the acquisition of the cottages was agreed in principle, and adjourned until the valuer's report had been received.

Mr. Gilmore elected to walk home. The meeting had revived memories that were not altogether pleasant. He had acted, naturally, for the council in the matter of Richard Penfold and had never felt too happy about it. Privately, he thought a law that enabled a person's home to be forcibly taken from him was iniquitous. But there was nothing he could do about it. That could only be done by an Act of Parliament.

He crossed the road towards the gates of the public gardens which were the council's pride and joy. They were not closed at night, and they constituted a short cut to Mr. Gilmore's house. Skirting the fountain and the ornamental pond that surrounded it, Charles Gilmore passed into the shadow of some large trees which, by some oversight, the council had failed to cut down. The path ran close to the massive trunks and emerged from their shadow to bisect a plot of grass, close-cut and dotted with geometrically shaped flower beds.

Mr. Gilmore should have emerged, too. But he didn't. The path across the lawn remained deserted.

In the shadow under the trees, a darker shadow stirred. It straightened up from something that lay on the concrete path, and walked quietly towards the open gates of the gardens.

* * *

In the corner of a small teashop, a hand holding a ballpoint pen hovered over the page of an open notebook. On the page was a short list of names, one of which had had a line drawn through it in red.

The hand holding the ballpoint pen carefully drew a line through the second name on the list.

6

The murder of Humphrey Gamble had been given a certain amount of prominence in the newspapers, but it was nothing in comparison to the sensational outburst that followed the discovery of the dead body of Charles Gilmore under similar circumstances.

The front pages broke out into a black rash of banner headlines, each featuring the unusual method of the murders.

'RED TAPE STRANGLES SOLICITORS'

'THE RED TAPE MURDERS'

'WHO IS THE RED TAPE MANIAC?'

Mr. Budd, after a wakeful and strenuous night, sat behind the desk in his office at Scotland Yard, his heavy jowls sagging more than usual from sheer weariness. Leek dozed uncomfortably on his hard chair, emitting every now and again an unmusical snore that jerked him back to wakefulness.

The body of Mr. Gilmore had been

discovered at a quarter to eleven on the previous night, lying on the path under some trees in the public gardens near his home. His death had been due to strangulation, caused by the length of red tape tightly knotted round his neck. The discovery had been made by a youth and his girlfriend on their way back from the cinema. The woman, who worked in a local tobacconist's and sweet shop, ran off to find a policeman, while her boyfriend stayed with the body.

Mr. Budd had just got into bed, looking forward to a good night's rest after his heavy day, when the telephone roused him to wakefulness. He listened resentfully to the news of the fresh murder, wearily dressed himself again, and waited for the police car that was on its way to pick him up. Accompanied by the photographers and fingerprint experts, the superintendent was at the scene of the crime within half an hour of the discovery of the body.

While the police doctor made his examination, and the photographers took pictures of the dead man's position from several angles, Mr. Budd interviewed the youth and the woman who had found it.

Lionel Bartlet was a mechanic who worked in a local garage. The woman's name was Elsie Pounds. They had very little information to offer. They had been walking home after the show at the local cinema was over, and had decided to go through the gardens. It wasn't a short cut, but they usually took a stroll round the gardens before going home. They had seen the dark form of Mr. Gilmore lying in the shadow of the trees, and had thought that he was either ill or drunk. They had been horrified when they had found what was actually the matter with him.

They had acted in a very sensible and level-headed way, and Mr. Budd congratulated them, found that they had already given their names and addresses to the constable, and allowed them to go home.

The constable, who had been joined by his inspector, was able to identify the dead man, whom he knew quite well. He was, apparently, a well-known figure in the district. His offices were in the high street, and he acted as legal adviser to the borough council. He lived with his wife and two children in a detached house in Fairmile Road, which was not far from the other entrance to the public gardens.

The news of his death had already been broken to his family. A police sergeant had been sent immediately, after the constable had notified his station.

By the time Mr. Budd had acquired all this information, and had a talk with the local inspector, a second police car arrived with a very miserable and disgruntled Leek. The sergeant, looking more melancholy and lugubrious than usual, had been sound asleep when the car had called at his lodgings to pick him up.

'Bit thick, this is,' he remarked unhappily. 'I was in me bed.'

'So was I,' snarled Mr. Budd. 'Maybe, if the murderer had known 'e was goin' to disturb us, he'd have postponed his killin' until the daytime.'

Leek blinked sleepily. 'Just like the

other, is it? Another red tape strangling, eh?'

'And a solicitor again. P'raps we'll find some sort of motive this time.'

The sergeant shook his head slowly. 'Looks ter me like the work of a loony.'

'Well, you ought to know what *that* looks like,' retorted Mr. Budd rudely.

Leek sighed. 'You will 'ave yer little joke,' he said. 'I was bein' serious.'

'So was I!' snapped his superior. 'I'm just goin' to make sure there's nothin' more to be learned here, an' then we're goin' to the dead man's house to have a word with his wife. Try not to fall into a coma while I'm away.' He left the sergeant standing unhappily by himself, and joined the group of men under the trees. The photographers were packing up their gear, and the fingerprint expert looked round as Mr. Budd approached, and shrugged his shoulders.

'Nothing for me here,' he said. 'The chappie who did this could scarcely have left his dabs on anything if he'd tried.'

Mr. Budd grunted. 'Never touched anythin' in the pockets. Can we move the body now, Doctor?'

The police doctor, who had come up while he had been talking, waved his hand. 'Go ahead. I've finished. Plain case of death by strangulation. No complications.'

Mr. Budd left the arrangements for the removal of the body to the local inspector, and went back to Leek. 'Come on,' he said. 'We'll go and have a word with the dead man's widow.'

He lumbered away towards the gate with the sergeant trailing behind him. It didn't take them long in the police car to reach the house. It was quite a pretentious place, standing back from the road in a well-kept garden. Judging from the appearance of his house, Gilmore's business had been a prosperous one.

Mrs. Gilmore opened the door herself, in answer to Mr. Budd's ring. She was a woman whose good looks were beginning to fade, and were certainly not enhanced by the ravages of grief visible in her swollen red-lidded eyes.

The stout superintendent introduced himself, apologising for disturbing her.

'It doesn't matter,' she said in a toneless voice. 'Please come in.' She led the way into a comfortably furnished lounge. An electric fire burned in the grate, and on a settee before it sat a young woman of about seventeen. She, too, had been crying. From her likeness to Mrs. Gilmore, Mr. Budd judged her to be the daughter.

'I'll be as brief as I can, ma'am,' said Mr. Budd. 'I'm very sorry to 'ave to bother you at all.'

'I've told you, it doesn't matter,' broke in Mrs. Gilmore wearily. 'It — it all seems so — so — ' Her voice trailed away and she began to cry, with long, shuddering sobs that shook her thin body.

The young woman sprang up from the settee and went to her, putting her arms round the shaking shoulders. 'Don't, mother — please, don't,' she entreated, though the tears were streaming down her own cheeks. 'Do you have to worry her now?' she asked, looking at Mr. Budd over the woman's shoulder.

'I'm afraid I must,' he answered sympathetically.

Mrs. Gilmore pushed her daughter gently away from her. 'I — I'm sorry,' she said with difficulty. 'I ought to — to have more control. The whole thing was such a shock — such a terrible shock.'

'I understand,' said Mr. Budd gently. 'It's only natural that you should feel upset.'

Mrs. Gilmore, with an effort, succeeded in mastering her emotion. With a handkerchief, she dried her eyes and blew her nose. 'What do you want?' she asked after a little while with more composure. 'How can I help you?'

Mr. Budd began a series of what were mostly routine questions. He elicited the fact that the Gilmores had been residents of Stonehurst Green nearly all their lives; that Charles Gilmore's business had been left him by his father; that it was an old established one with a very large clientele; that the Gilmores had a great many friends not only in the district but elsewhere, that so far as Mrs. Gilmore knew, there was no motive for anyone wishing to kill her husband. In addition to this information, he learned that Mr.

Gilmore had, that evening, returned home from the office at five o'clock, which was his usual time; that he had had his tea, and written a letter to their son, Colin, aged fourteen, who was at boarding school. That he had then examined some papers he had brought back with him from the office until just before six forty-five, when he left the house to attend a council meeting at the Town Hall. From this he had never returned. And that was all.

Mr. Budd obtained the addresses of several members of the borough council, and took his departure, glad to leave the house where tragedy had struck so unexpectedly.

He hadn't been very hopeful that he would discover anything from Mrs. Gilmore that would throw a light on the reason for her husband's murder. Either there was no sane reason behind the red tape murderer's activities, or it was something a lot deeper than was likely to come out by an inquiry into the past of the victims. In this, as it turned out, he was wrong. From the dead man's house,

Mr. Budd, accompanied by the yawning Leek, drove to the abode of Councillor Cranbourne.

Councillor Cranbourne was in bed, and took quite a lot of rousing. By the time this was accomplished, Councillor Cranbourne was not in the best of tempers. He demanded to know, with several unprintable adjectives — unprintable even in these enlightened days — why he had been disturbed at that hour?

When Mr. Budd told him, he was horrified. 'Good God!' he exclaimed. 'Gilmore? It's impossible. Strangled — in the public gardens? Bless my soul, what will happen next?'

The superintendent wasn't quite sure whether it was the fact that Gilmore had been strangled, or whether it was because this had taken place in the public gardens, that caused Councillor Cranbourne so much consternation. He didn't, however, pursue the point, but put the question that had made him seek Councillor Cranbourne at such a late hour.

'What time did he leave the meeting . . . ?' Councillor Cranbourne frowned. 'Let me see, now. The meeting ended at ten o'clock. We talked afterwards for some time. It would be about a quarter past ten when he left — '

'Did you say goodnight to him in the street?' asked Mr. Budd. 'Did you leave the Town Hall together?'

'Yes,' said Councillor Cranbourne. 'I went up the road to the car park for my car.'

'How far from the Town Hall is the entrance to these gardens?'

'Not very far — about five minutes' walk.'

'Did you pass Mr. Gilmore after you'd got in your car?'

'Yes, I did.'

'Did you see anyone behind him?' asked Mr. Budd. 'Someone who might've been followin' him?'

'I don't think so.' Councillor Cranbourne shook his head. 'I don't remember seeing anyone.'

Gilmore had left the Town Hall at approximately ten-fifteen, thought Mr.

Budd. The body had been found at a quarter to eleven. Roughly half an hour later. During that short period, the murderer had struck.

He put the usual routine questions to Councillor Cranbourne, and received what he had come to regard as the usual routine answers. Hardly disappointed, for he expected nothing else, he left the still horrified councillor to return to his rest, and sought out the others on his list.

The reaction from all of them was the same. They were surprised and horrified at the news, but could suggest no reason why anyone should wish to kill Gilmore. The general opinion, taking into consideration the murder of Mr. Humphrey Gamble in similar circumstances, was that it was the work of a homicidal maniac.

Mr. Budd, weary but indefatigable, went to the local police station. There must be put into operation immediately, he ordered, an inquiry to find out who was abroad in Stonehurst Green the previous night, between ten-fifteen and ten forty-five. Exactly where they had been at that time, and, if in the vicinity of the Town Hall, or the public gardens; what they had been doing; and who they had seen.

'It'll probably lead to nothin',' he said pessimistically, 'but there's just about one chance in a thousand that someone may have seen the murderer an' can give us a description of him.'

'It's going to be a pretty hefty job,' remarked the local inspector dubiously.

'I know,' grunted Mr. Budd. 'You'd better get started as soon as possible.'

The superintendent's activities were by no means over when he was driven back to Scotland Yard. There were a considerable number of details to be attended to — all the purely routine work that attaches to an inquiry into wilful murder. Dawn was breaking coldly before he had finished setting into motion the various lines of inquiry that might unearth one small detail from which could be patiently built up a case against — someone.

The murder had been discovered in time for the news to reach Fleet Street before the deadline, and all the newspapers carried sensational headlines on their front pages.

The *Morning Mail* was no exception. Mr. Sorbet, the news editor of that enterprising journal, with his subs, had worked feverishly to change the entire format of the front page just before the paper was put to bed. He cursed the fact that Peter Ashton, his star crime reporter, was in Paris over another assignment, but he took immediate steps to rectify this. The night lines across the Channel hummed with activity. Peter Ashton was found, after some trouble, in a night club in Montmartre, and was ordered to drop everything and catch the first available plane back to England. He arrived at London Airport in the early hours of that morning, where a car was waiting to rush him to the offices of the *Morning Mail*.

'I suppose the money you spent in that night club'll go down on your expense sheet?' grunted a weary Mr. Sorbet, scowling ferociously. He was in reality the mildest of men, but his expression had been known to scare the teaboy out of his wits. 'Well, you won't get it.'

'Considering I was there in the interests of the paper,' retorted Peter, 'I most certainly shall! Now, what's the idea of dragging me back here at this unholy hour, eh? I'd got a big story lined up.'

'There's a bigger one waiting for you,' said the news editor; and he proceeded to tell him briefly what it was. 'Go after this red tape killer,' he ended. 'Find out who he is, and what's at the back of these stranglings. I want an exclusive story.'

Peter Ashton looked interested. 'Lawyers strangled with red tape,' he said with a whistle. 'It really sounds like something.'

'There's a big story somewhere. It's up to you to find it. Superintendent Budd is in charge of the case. You get on with him pretty well, don't you?'

Peter nodded. He remembered the affair of the Silver Horseshoe and that other queer business of the Football Pool Murders. He had met his wife in the former. He had worked with Mr. Budd on both cases, but it was several months since he had last seen him. 'I'll go and hunt him up,' he said, and chuckled.

'What's amusing you?' demanded Mr. Sorbet suspiciously.

'I was thinking of Leek. He always gives me a good laugh. Poor old Leek; he tried to make money backing horses and filling up football pool coupons. I must say, he very nearly pulled off a big win on them. Only he forgot to post.'

'Never mind the reminiscences,' snarled Mr. Sorbet. 'Get busy!'

Peter paid a brief visit to his home, to the astonishment of his wife, who was still in bed and was under the impression that he was still in Paris.

'When did *you* come back?' she asked sleepily, sitting up and clutching the eiderdown round her.

'On the first plane this morning,' answered Peter, kissing her. 'You can settle down and go to sleep again, darling. I'm not stopping.'

'Nonsense,' she exclaimed. 'I'll get up and make some tea.'

'Well, I won't say no to that. But you'll have to be quick. I've only got about ten minutes.'

'Where are you going?' she called as he made a dash for the bathroom. 'Back to Paris?'

'No,' he called back from the passage. 'I'll be home again later.'

She heard him turn on the bath water, and got out of bed. It was all very exciting being married to a newspaper reporter, she thought as she pulled on her dressing-gown, but life was apt to be a little disconcerting on occasions.

By the time Peter had shaved and had a hasty bath, the tea was ready. He gulped it down quickly, nearly scalding himself in the process.

'I suppose it's no good asking you what this is all about,' said Marjory.

'Haven't time to tell you now. I'll tell you all about it when I see you again.'

'When will that be?'

'I don't know — soon,' he replied, and was gone.

★ ★ ★

Mr. Budd was dozing at his desk when the messenger brought in the printed blank, which everyone calling at Scotland Yard has to fill in with their name and business, and who they wished to see, before they could be admitted. He took it in his fingers and glanced sleepily at the name.

'All right,' he grunted, 'shoot him up.' He looked across at the slumbering Leek. 'You'd better pull yerself together. We've got a visitor.'

The sergeant continued to sleep peacefully.

'Wake up!' cried Mr. Budd, bringing his fist down with a crash on the desk.

Leek woke up. He shot out of his chair like a stone from a catapult, lost his balance, and only saved himself from falling by clutching wildly at the edge of the desk. 'What's 'appened?' he demanded. 'Somethin' exploded right under me nose.'

'I wish it had,' growled Mr. Budd unsympathetically. 'It might've stopped you makin' all them weird noises. Come on, wake up! Ashton's on his way up to see us.'

'I wasn't asleep,' said Leek, rubbing his eyes. 'I was thinkin'.'

'If that's the way you do it,' said Mr. Budd, 'it's not surprisin' that yer thoughts are such a mess.'

Before the melancholy sergeant could think of a suitable reply, Peter Ashton was shown in.

'Hello, hello,' he greeted cheerily. 'Both the great minds on the job, eh?' He shook hands with the superintendent and eyed him critically. 'You're putting on weight,' he said. 'And how's the redoubtable Leek, eh? Been backing any more horses or winning the pools lately?'

'I've given up them frivolous things,' answered Leek with dignity. 'I'm scientific now.'

Peter Ashton stared at him in astonishment. 'What do you mean, scientific?'

Mr. Budd snorted. 'He means he's got bitten with a worse bug than ever,' he growled. 'He's taken up 'ypnotism.'

'Hypnotism?' repeated Peter incredulously. 'Oh, no!'

'Oh, yes,' said Mr. Budd. 'Nobody's safe from the power of his eye these days. He tried to put the 'fluence on me the other mornin'. It was a remarkable demonstration.'

'Do you mean he actually put you to sleep?'

'The only person he's any good at puttin' to sleep is himself. No, he didn't put me to sleep, Mr. Ashton, but his antics would've frightened a witch doctor! I thought he'd really gone barmy at last.'

'You don't understand these things,' interposed the sergeant, shaking his head. 'I've read a lot o' books about it.'

'You could read a lot of books about ballet dancin',' broke in Mr. Budd, 'but you couldn't do it.'

Peter burst out laughing. The picture of the thin and miserable-looking Leek attempting a ballet dance, conjured up by the superintendent's remark, struck him as particularly ludicrous.

Leek blinked at him with a slightly injured expression. 'It's all very well ter laugh,' he said, 'but this 'ypnotism is doin' a lot o' good. Doctors are usin' it to bring babies into the world.'

'If I catch you tryin' to bring any babies into the world,' threatened Mr. Budd sternly, 'I'll go straight to the chief commissioner.'

'You'd better come along and hypnotise old Sorbet before he sees my expense account,' said Peter. 'He'll need it! Now,' he continued seriously, turning to Mr. Budd, 'what's all this red tape business, eh?'

'So that's what you've come for, is it?' remarked Mr. Budd, yawning. 'I thought we'd got rid of you for a bit.'

'They hauled me back when the news of the second murder broke. What can you tell me about it?'

'What do you know already?'

Peter shrugged his shoulders. 'Not much,' he answered candidly. He told the superintendent what Mr. Sorbet had told him that morning.

'Then you know as much as I do,' grunted Mr. Budd disgustedly. 'I can't tell you anything, because I don't *know* anything. Two people have been killed, both lawyers, an' both strangled with a bit of red tape. That's all. There's no apparent motive why they should've been killed, or why the murderer should have used a bit of red tape to do the job.'

'Maniac with a grudge against the law?' suggested Peter.

'Maybe,' said Mr. Budd, yawning again. 'And maybe not. If not, there must be somethin' that links these two people together somewhere. But I can't find it. I've established that Gamble an' Gilmore didn't know each other — '

'But they were both in the same profession,' said Peter, frowning. 'They were both solicitors.'

'An' both their names began with the initial G,' augmented Mr. Budd.

'Does that mean anything to you?' asked Peter Ashton quickly, but Mr. Budd only shook his head.

'Nothin' at all,' he declared. 'I'm only just mentionin' it as a fact. Nothin' means anythin' to me,' he added despondently. 'I can't get a line to work on.'

'If you'd let me try the effect of 'ypnotism on Miss Emily Gamble . . . ' began Leek.

'We'd both've been chucked out o' the Yard,' snarled Mr. Budd.

'Good Lord, he didn't want to do *that*,

did he?' exclaimed Peter, aghast.

'You got ter keep up with the times,' said the sergeant defensively. 'Modern methods, that's what you want 'ere.'

'Go an' tell the home secretary,' snapped his superior. 'I've got enough on my plate without any trouble from you.'

'There's absolutely no clue to the identity of the murderer?' asked Peter.

'Not even the ghost of one. He might be anybody among a few million people. It's goin' ter be a nice job pickin' him out.' He sighed and stretched himself wearily. 'So you see, there's nothin' I can give you.'

'Cheer up,' encouraged Peter. 'We'll find something. Tell me what you know about Gamble and Gilmore — what sort of men were they? Who were their friends, their relations? All about 'em.'

Rather dispiritedly, for he was very tired, Mr. Budd complied. The reporter listened quietly without comment until he had finished.

'There certainly doesn't seem to be much there,' he remarked. 'This is the second time that Stonehurst Green's going to achieve prominence in the press.'

'What d'you mean?' asked Mr. Budd sharply.

'The borough council came in for a lot of unpleasant criticism over that rather nasty business, a year ago. Don't you remember it? A chap called Penfold shot himself because the council took away his home by compulsory purchase. He'd spent all his savings on it. They offered him a ridiculous sum — wanted to build a new road, and his house was in the way.'

Mr. Budd, suddenly very alert and wakeful, sat up with a jerk. 'Tell me all you know about it,' he demanded. 'Maybe this is what I've been lookin' for — a jumpin'-off place.'

7

Peter Ashton's memory failed to supply all the details connected with the tragedy of Richard Penfold, but he was able to give the interested Mr. Budd the gist of the matter.

'We've got to get the full facts o' that business,' he declared, rubbing his head energetically. 'It may have a lot of bearing on this red tape killin'.'

'I can get you all the facts that were known at the time,' said Peter. 'The back files of the *Morning Mail* 'ull give you those. It created quite a bit of a sensation, you know.'

'I remember somethin' about it now,' said the superintendent. 'I should've remembered more, but I was very busy when it happened. I didn't rightly take much notice of it at the time. Did this feller have a wife?'

'Penfold?' Peter shook his head. 'No, he wasn't married. But he was going to be.

That's why he'd built the bungalow — as a home for his future wife.'

'Who was she?' asked Mr. Budd, and again Peter shook his head.

'I don't remember. It'll be in the files. We had an interview with her after the tragedy.'

'What about Penfold's relations? Father, mother, brothers, sisters?'

'Can't tell you. I know who probably can, though. Henson. He covered the story for the *Mail*. He'd know all about it.'

'I'd like to have a word with him, and take a look at those files. I'm very much obliged to you, Mr. Ashton. You may've put me on to somethin'.'

'Your idea being,' remarked Peter, 'that some relative, or someone closely connected with Penfold, is out for a spot of revenge, eh?'

'Somethin' of the sort. This feller, Gilmore, was the lawyer for the council.'

'But Gamble wasn't,' interposed Peter quickly. 'He wasn't connected with the Penfold case at all.'

'No, that's true,' said Mr. Budd,

frowning. 'Maybe he *did* have a connection that we don't know about . . . '

'Never twist your facts to suit your theory,' admonished Peter Ashton severely. 'The first principles of detection. I'm surprised at you!'

'I haven't got a theory, so I couldn't twist anythin'. I'm just goin' to follow up an idea an' see how far it gets me. The bungalow, or whatever it was, has been pulled down, I suppose?'

'I don't know,' said Peter. 'It's no good asking *me* all these questions. I only just recollect the bare facts, that's all.'

'All right, all right. Keep your hair on,' said Mr. Budd testily. 'I'll do all the findin' out.'

'We'll work together.'

The big man looked a trifle dubious. 'Well, I don't know about that . . . '

'We've done it before,' argued the reporter, 'and it turned out a very good partnership.'

'Hm. I s'pose there's somethin' in that,' admitted Mr. Budd grudgingly. 'But you're not printin' anythin' in that rag you work for without my permission.'

'Did I ever? All I want is a twenty-four hour beat before you release any information to the rest of the press. All right?'

'I don't mind agreein' to that.'

'Good! Then we may as well get started. You'd better come along to the offices of the *Mail*, and we'll have a look at the files. We shan't need Leek.'

The sergeant's long face brightened. 'I could do with a bit of sleep,' he began, but Mr. Budd interrupted him.

'We all could,' he said, 'but we're not gettin' it! You're goin' along to Stonehurst Green to see what information you can get about this Penfold business. Get hold of the people still livin' there who knew him. I want to know everythin' you can find out.'

'It'll all be in the newspapers,' said Leek. 'There don't seem any sense in my goin' over the same ground.'

'You might hit on somethin' that the newspapers overlooked. Anyway, that's where you're goin'. An' don't try any o' this hypnotic stuff, or you'll land yerself in trouble.'

Leek sighed. 'All right. I'll do what I can.'

★ ★ ★

The story of Richard Penfold's tragedy, as reported in the *Morning Mail* at the time, was in some respects clear enough.

Penfold had been an officer in the Blankshire Regiment during the Second World War. He had risen to the rank of major; had been through the hell of Dunkirk, where he had been wounded. After recovering in hospital, he had served again overseas, and had been among the first to land on the beaches on D-day. His nerves had suffered badly from the effects of his war service. In company with a number of others in a similar condition, he had spent several months in a clinic after the war was finally over.

After leaving the clinic and getting his discharge from the army, he found himself a job with a firm of electric switch manufacturers as sales manager. It was a reasonably well-paid job, and although he suffered from fits of depression occasionally, and was apt to lose his temper very easily, the firm were quite pleased with him.

It was during this period that he met a woman named Lucy Bristow who worked in an accountant's office in Clapham, fell in love with her, and they became engaged. Penfold had always been a sober, careful man, and with his gratuity, had managed to save nearly four thousand pounds. His salary with the electric switch company was fifteen hundred a year, and after consultation with Lucy Bristow, he decided to use his savings for the purpose of building a house. He selected Stonehurst Green, found a reasonably sized piece of land, bought it, and had his bungalow built. He had taken a tremendous pride in the place, spending all his spare time working on the garden, to provide a suitable setting for his 'ideal home'.

A year after it was completed, the blow fell. Stonehurst Green Borough Council planned a new road which would bypass a dangerous corner where there was considerable traffic congestion. Unfortunately, the new road meant the demolition of Richard Penfold's bungalow. He was served with a compulsory purchase notice, the price offered being totally inadequate. He refused to sell, and took the matter to court. But as the law stood, he had no chance of winning his case. It was decided against him, Charles Gilmore appearing for the council. Penfold appealed, but his appeal was dismissed. He was given six months to vacate the premises.

The worry of it all brought on a recurrence of his nervous disability. He neglected his job, and in spite of the sympathy which everybody felt for him, was eventually asked to resign. The wedding was postponed. Penfold was now almost completely broke. The two hundred and fifty pounds offered by the council was nothing compared to his loss. On the verge of a complete nervous breakdown, and feeling incapable of starting all over again, Penfold, on the eve of the day on which he was supposed to vacate his home, went out into his garden and shot himself with his service revolver.

The resultant outcry had reached Parliament, and questions were asked in the House. An Act was passed empowering local authorities to pay more in the future. But the iniquities of compulsory purchase still remained law.

'Not a very pleasant business,' grunted Mr. Budd when he had digested the various reports in the back numbers of the *Morning Mail*. 'There's one queer thing. There's no mention of any relations. Didn't this poor chap, Penfold, have any?'

'Apparently not,' said Peter.

'They didn't attend the inquest,' remarked Mr. Budd. 'Only this woman, Lucy Bristow. If he'd had a father, or a mother, or a brother, surely they'd've come too? It's funny he didn't have *anybody*.'

Peter thought it was peculiar. 'Perhaps he was an orphan?' he suggested.

'Maybe. If he hadn't any close relative, it rather knocks our idea on the head, doesn't it? We're supposin' that somebody started this red tape business because of what happened to Penfold. But if there wasn't anybody close enough to care, that theory looks like goin' west.'

'There's the woman,' said Peter.

Mr. Budd shook his head. 'Can you see a woman goin' about stranglin' lawyers with a bit of red tape? I can't. She'd've chosen some other an' easier method — like poison. I wonder where this woman is now?'

'Let's go and hunt up Henson,' said Peter. 'He may be able to tell us a lot more than was printed.'

'He couldn't tell us much less. There's nothin' here to help us.'

They ran Henson to earth in the saloon bar of a pub halfway down Fleet Street. He was a small bald-headed man with a florid face and twinkling eyes behind thick-lensed glasses.

'Well, well,' he exclaimed as he saw Peter. 'I thought you were enjoying yourself in Paris. What happened?'

'I was recalled early this morning. Been assigned to cover these red tape murders.'

'Oh,' said Henson, 'you're on that, are

110

you? I should say you'd got all your work cut out there. What are you having?'

'Beer,' said Peter, and he introduced Mr. Budd. 'He drinks beer, too,' he added.

Henson ordered three pints of bitter. 'What do you want me for?' he asked.

'How do you know we want you for anything?' demanded the reporter.

Henson shrugged his shoulders. 'Obvious, my dear Watson,' he replied with a grin. 'You come into this bar and you look quickly round. You're looking for someone. You spot me and you come straight over. I'm therefore the person you're looking for. Simple.'

Peter laughed. 'Well, you're right. We want some information. Do you remember that business at Stonehurst Green? Penfold and his bungalow?'

'So that's it, eh?' Henson paid for the drinks which the barmaid set down on the counter. 'Are you suggesting that it's got anything to do with these murders?'

'We're just following up an inquiry,' said Mr. Budd. 'The man who was murdered last night, Charles Gilmore, was mixed up in the Penfold affair, an' so we'd like to know all about it.'

Henson took a draught of beer. 'I see. Well, I can tell you a good bit about it. Nasty. I think most people's sympathies were with Penfold, although the chap needn't have behaved so foolishly. The loss of the bungalow wasn't enough to justify killing himself.'

'That depends how *he* looked at it,' said Peter. 'I gather that it meant a lot to him.'

'Oh, it did. I saw him before he shot himself, you know. I had three interviews with him while he was fighting to try and save his property. Neurotic type.'

'Did he 'ave any relations?' asked Mr. Budd.

'Ah, I see the line,' said Henson, nodding his bald head sagaciously. ''Fraid it's a wash-out, though. So far as I know, he didn't have any.'

'Did he tell you so?' said the superintendent.

'Well, he didn't actually say so. But he never mentioned any, and certainly

nobody came forward claiming relationship with him.'

'What happened to the bungalow?'
inquired Peter. 'Was it demolished?'

'Yes, a month or so after Penfold's
death. The new road's nearly completed.'

'Who got the money?' said Mr. Budd
curiously.

'The money? Oh, you mean the two
hundred and fifty pounds from the
council? That interested *me*. I took the
trouble to find out. It was Lucy Bristow.
Penfold left a will leaving everything to
her. The bungalow became her property
after his death, so they paid the money to
her.'

'Where's this Lucy Bristow now?' asked
Mr. Budd.

'That I can't tell you,' said Henson,
finishing his beer. 'She shouldn't be
difficult to find.'

There was very little more to be
learned from Henson. What they had
learned didn't add much to what they
already knew. As yet, there was nothing to
even hint at a clue to the red tape
murderer. It was quite possible that they

were on the wrong track altogether, but since there was no other track visible, it was worth following it to the end.

Peter bought another round of drinks, and then he and Mr. Budd left Henson at the bar and went out into Fleet Street.

'I must go to the office,' said the reporter, 'and churn out something to follow-up this morning's news.'

'You be careful what yer say,' warned Mr. Budd.

Peter laughed. 'Don't worry. Long practice has made me a past master in the art of writing a sensational column all about nothing at all! It won't please Sorbet, but it'll satisfy the public.'

He left Mr. Budd outside the *Morning Mail* building, and that weary man made his way to Clapham to find the firm of accountants who had employed Lucy Bristow. He found it in the high street, a set of offices over a tailor's shop.

The outer office was presided over by a young woman. In answer to his inquiry, she looked at him blankly. 'Lucy Bristow?' she said nasally. 'Can't say I've ever 'eard the name. I 'aven't been here long, you see.'

Mr. Budd produced his card. 'Take that in to Mr. Alterman, an' say I'd like a word with him.'

She looked at the card, and her eyes widened. 'Detective, are you? What's the trouble? Anything excitin'?'

'There's no trouble,' answered Mr. Budd reassuringly. 'I'm just makin' an inquiry, that's all.'

It was quite obvious that she didn't believe him. In a flutter of excitement, she got up and went to a door at the other end of the office. On this she tapped and entered. After a moment or so, a thin dark man came out, holding Mr. Budd's card in his hand.

'You wish to see me?' he asked.

'That's right, sir,' said Mr. Budd. 'I'm anxious to trace a woman who used to work here — a Miss Lucy Bristow. Can you tell me her address?'

Over the dark man's face passed a faint expression of relief. Mr. Alterman had a skeleton in his cupboard somewhere, thought Mr. Budd, who had seen that expression before, and had been afraid it was going to rattle.

'Ah, yes. Lucy Bristow,' said Mr. Alterman. 'She was mixed up in that shocking affair at Stonehurst Green. Engaged to the chap who shot himself, eh?'

'That's right, sir.'

'She left here soon after on account of illness. The shock of that chap's death, you know. I was sorry to lose her.'

'Have you any idea where she is now, sir?'

'I can tell you her address, when she worked here. Look it up, Miss Stiller, will you? It's in the file under 'staff'.'

Miss Stiller, who had been watching and listening in the hope that something sensational would happen, sniffed disappointedly and moved over to a filing cabinet against the wall.

'She lived with her parents, I believe,' volunteered Mr. Alterman while Miss Stiller languidly began her search. 'Somewhere near the Common, I think. Haven't you found it yet, Miss Stiller?'

Apparently she had not.

'Here, let me look,' said Mr. Alterman irritably. 'That's the wrong drawer, anyway.' He pulled out the drawer beneath the one in which Miss Stiller had been futilely burrowing and took out a card. 'Here it is,' he continued. 'Sixty-eight, Manderin Road, North Side.'

'Thanks very much, sir,' said Mr. Budd, and he copied the address down in his notebook.

'No trouble, I hope?' said Mr. Alterman in the tone of one who hopes quite the reverse.

'No, sir. Just a routine inquiry, that's all.'

Leaving the accountant's office, he was driven to the Common and along North Side. After a little trouble, he discovered Manderin Road at the farther end. It was a quiet road of small neat houses, nearly all exactly alike. There was no front garden to any of them, only a narrow strip of concrete enclosed by a low brick wall. Number sixty-eight was on the right-hand side at the far end, almost the last house in the road.

Mr. Budd knocked. There was no reply

for quite a long time, and he was in the act of raising his hand to knock again when he heard footsteps approaching from inside the house. The door was opened, and a stout woman with greying hair looked at him inquiringly.

'Sorry to disturb you, ma'am,' said Mr. Budd politely. 'But does Miss Lucy Bristow live here?'

'She's not here now. What is it you want?'

'I wanted to see Miss Bristow. Are you a relation of hers?'

'I'm her mother.'

Mr. Budd explained the reason for his visit — at least, he explained part of it. He made no mention of the red tape murders. He merely said that he wanted to ask Lucy Bristow a few questions concerning the death of Richard Penfold.

'What for?' demanded Mrs. Bristow harshly. 'There's nothing can be done. Why rake it all up again? Dick Penfold was a weak fool! He was treated very badly, I'll agree, but he should have faced it out, not done what he did. He had a good job with a good salary. He could have pulled himself round again. The whole thing nearly killed my daughter.'

'You knew Richard Penfold quite well?' broke in Mr. Budd gently. 'Did he ever talk about his relations?'

'Come to think of it, I never heard him mention any relatives. Why do you want to know?'

'Just a matter for the records,' replied Mr. Budd evasively. 'Would it be possible to see your daughter?'

'She's down in the country. She hasn't recovered yet from that awful business.'

Mr. Budd asked for the address.

'Well, I don't know that I ought to give it to you,' said Mrs. Bristow, reluctantly. 'I don't want her worried.'

'I'm afraid, I'll have to insist, ma'am.'

The woman hesitated. He thought she was going to refuse, but she didn't.

'She's staying with a school friend at Camelford, in Cornwall,' she said, and gave him the address which he noted down. 'I hope, if you see her, that it won't upset her.'

Mr. Budd assured her that he would do his best to see that it didn't, and took his departure. As he walked slowly back to the police car, which he had stopped farther up the road, he saw a man coming towards him on the other side of the street. There was something familiar about him, and Mr. Budd stopped in the shelter of the car and watched the approaching figure without himself being seen.

The man crossed the road and entered the short tiled path leading to the front door of number sixty-eight. As he raised his hand to knock, Mr. Budd was sure.

It was Timothy Smithson!

8

Timothy Smithson! And he was paying a visit to the Bristows!

Mr. Budd hesitated, with the open door of the police car in his hand. Should he go back and find out what Smithson was doing there?

He decided that he wouldn't. He'd wait, but Timothy Smithson definitely merited further inquiry.

On the way back to Scotland Yard, Mr. Budd's mind was busily occupied. Hunched up in the back seat of the car, his eyes closed and his hands clasped loosely over his stomach, he reviewed the situation.

If Timothy Smithson knew the Bristows, then he also knew about the tragedy of Richard Penfold. And the late Charles Gilmore's connection with it. Was *this* the link between Gamble and Gilmore that he'd been seeking? Was Smithson the unknown murderer?

He was, certainly, the only person to benefit from the death of Humphrey Gamble. Under Gamble's will, he inherited not only the business but the bulk of Gamble's money as well. That was a clear enough motive, so far as Humphrey Gamble was concerned, but it didn't cover the murder of Charles Gilmore. If that was in some way mixed up with Richard Penfold's suicide, then what motive had Timothy Smithson for that?

You couldn't have it both ways. If Timothy Smithson had killed Gamble for the business and the money, then there was nothing in the theory that the red tape murderer was someone who was taking revenge for what had happened to Penfold. But Smithson was obviously connected, somehow, with Mrs. Bristow, and fairly closely connected, too. Mr. Budd had seen him go straight in when the woman answered the door. There had been no time for any introductory remarks. Which meant that he was well known to Mrs. Bristow.

Could it be that he was a relation, or, perhaps, a relation of the late Richard

Penfold? It seemed wildly improbable that he could be the latter. If he had been a relation of Penfold's, why hadn't he come forward at the inquest? So far as inquiries had gone, there was no evidence that Penfold had any relations living. Nobody seemed to have heard any mention of such a thing. Penfold himself had never talked about any relations, either distant or otherwise. But it might well be that Smithson was related to the Bristows.

Well, supposing he was, Mr. Budd mused. Where did that get you? Instead of clearing anything up, it got you into a worse tangle. It was straining the credulities too far to suppose that there were two separate and distinct motives for the murders — one for gain and one for revenge. Unless the gain had been incidental. Supposing Smithson had been unaware that Gamble had left a will in his favour? Supposing he had killed Gamble because he was, in some way or other, mixed up in the Penfold business — what then?

The answer was that there was nothing

to show that Gamble *had* been mixed up in the Penfold business. There was nothing as yet to show that the Penfold business had anything to do with the motive for the red tape murders, either. It was a line that had naturally suggested itself, but there might be nothing in it after all. It was a fatal mistake to go jumping at conclusions without hard facts to back them up. You could land yourself in a quagmire that way.

But it was a peculiar coincidence that Timothy Smithson seemed to be on fairly intimate terms with Mrs. Bristow. If it *was* a coincidence. *Now we're back where we started*, thought Mr. Budd. *It's no good going round and round in circles. The thing to do at this stage is to collect all the facts. We can juggle 'em into a pattern later.*

When he reached his office, he took off his coat and hat, and sitting down at his desk, pulled the telephone towards him. He asked the switchboard to get him through to Camelford police station. When he was connected, he spoke to the superintendent in charge of the C.I.D.

The result of his call was to send a man to the address where Lucy Bristow was staying, with instruction to find out from her everything she could tell him concerning Richard Penfold.

That was that. The next thing was to pay a visit to the offices of Messrs. Gamble, Chalkit, Gamble and Gamble, and have a word with Timothy Smithson. Mr. Budd concluded that the managing clerk would hardly have had time to get back yet, so he went round to the little teashop in Whitehall where he was accustomed to eat a frugal meal of buttered toast and tea.

The lunch hour rush was over and he had the place almost to himself. In the old days they used to *bring* him his tea and toast, but now he had to fetch it himself.

He was steadily munching his buttered toast at a secluded table when a man came in and bought a cup of coffee. As he turned away from the counter to find a table, Mr. Budd recognised him. It was Mr. Grindthorpe. The stout lawyer saw him at the same time, and his round and cherubic face became wreathed in smiles.

'Hello,' he said, coming over. 'Mind if I sit with you? Curious coincidence finding you here. I was only just thinking about you. Saw in the papers this morning about this other murder. Must be a lunatic, eh?' Mr. Grindthorpe sat down and began to stir his coffee vigorously. 'How are you getting on with the case? Any fresh clues?'

Mr. Budd, his mouth full of toast, contented himself by shaking his head.

'Difficult thing, when you haven't got a reasonable motive to help you,' said Mr. Grindthorpe. 'If this red tape chappie is a homicidal maniac, you're going to have a bit of trouble in finding him. Except for this kink against solicitors, he's probably normal, eh? Might be anybody.'

Mr. Budd swallowed his toast. 'We can't be sure that we've got a maniac to deal with, yet,' he said.

Mr. Grindthorpe gave him a sharp glance. 'Other ideas, eh? Got on to something that might be a motive?' He sipped at his coffee. 'Must be a peculiar one. The murderer's got to have a reason for using red tape, eh? Otherwise, why use it?'

'Maybe it was easier to get hold of than anythin' else.'

The lawyer's eyes narrowed shrewdly. 'You mean it could be someone in the legal profession, eh? Well, that's an idea. 'Set a thief to catch a thief, set a lawyer to kill a lawyer,' eh?'

'I haven't gone as far as that yet. Did you know this man who was killed last night?'

'Gilmore?' Mr. Grindthorpe shook his head. 'No — saw in the paper he had a wife and two children. Terrible for them, eh? Always worse for the people who are left, you know. They've got to go on living.'

Mr. Budd nodded. 'Yes, you're right there. Do you remember that business about Penfold?'

'Penfold . . . ' Mr. Grindthorpe wrinkled his forehead. 'Why, of course! You mean the fellow who shot himself? I should say I do remember. Used to discuss it with Gamble. Nasty-tasting business, eh? Within the law, though.'

'You don't agree with it?' said Mr. Budd.

The lawyer shook his head emphatically. 'I don't agree with any law that enables a man to be done out of his rights. That's what happened to Penfold, you know? It's happened to a lot of other people, too, and will happen to a lot more, until they alter it. It shouldn't be possible to compel anyone to give up something that rightly belongs to them, eh? It amounts to legal robbery.'

'That's a queer sentiment, comin' from a lawyer,' remarked Mr. Budd, wiping his mouth with his handkerchief.

Mr. Grindthorpe chuckled. 'I feel rather strongly about injustice. Law and justice don't always go together, you know. Maybe that's why the statue of justice on the top of the Old Bailey is blindfolded.'

'Did Mr. Gamble feel the same way?'

'He was more old-fashioned. The law was the *law*. He was interested in the Penfold case, naturally.'

'Why 'naturally'?' broke in Mr. Budd, suddenly very alert.

'Didn't you know?' asked Mr. Grindthorpe, looking surprised. 'It was Gamble who sold Richard Penfold the land on which he built his bungalow.'

★ ★ ★

Sergeant Leek, despite his numerous peculiarities, was a very able man at his job. Mr. Budd was aware of this and bore with his subordinate's eccentricities. There were others in Scotland Yard, however, who were not so patient. Leek was only efficient when he chose to exert himself, and since this was seldom, he had achieved the unenviable reputation of being born lazy. This was true. He did all he could to dodge work, but when it was inevitable, he performed his allotted task to the best of his ability.

The job he had been sent to do at Stonehurst Green he would gladly have avoided if he could. But as he couldn't, he decided to make the best of it. It was going to be a bit difficult, he thought. Nearly all the information that was likely to be known about Richard Penfold must have come out at the time of his suicide. The newspaper reporters must have scraped the bone clean. And the information that Mr. Budd wanted was something that *hadn't* been divulged at the time.

Always the same, it was, thought the sergeant lugubriously as he mooched along the high street, trying to make up his mind where to begin his investigations. The really tedious jobs always came *his* way. If it was a question of getting soaked to the skin in the pouring rain, watching some house or other; if it meant trailing someone for miles and miles in the scorching sun, the job was given to *him*. It was the same if there was any trouble. *He* fell into it. He remembered the time when that feller he'd been after had shoved him down a disused drain.

The first thing to do in the job he was on at present was to decide where he would find the most likely source of information. The idea of a public house presented itself, but he discarded that at once. There were too many of them in Stonehurst Green. That would have been all right in a village. The next best thing was a shop, but it had to be the right sort of shop. The shops in the high street would be no good. What he wanted was a small shop, a tobacconist's, or a kind of general store — somewhere that Penfold might have used.

Leek left the main thoroughfare of Stonehurst Green and explored the side streets. There were rows of houses in most of them, but no shops of any sort. The sergeant walked up one street and down another until he began to feel not only tired and hungry, but thoroughly disgruntled. This was the sort of thing he hated. He wondered what Mr. Budd was doing at that moment. Sitting comfortably at his desk, thinking, he supposed. He certainly wasn't wearing his boots out looking for needles in haystacks, and non-existent haystacks at that.

He hadn't the remotest idea where he was. He'd come a very long way from the high street, and that was all he knew. Stonehurst Green was one of those places that seemed to straggle all over the map. It wasn't much good turning back — he wasn't quite sure, by now, where 'back' lay. The only thing to do was to go on.

He came to the end of a long uninteresting avenue and turned into a short street that ran along at the end of it. And the first thing he saw was a small shop on the corner. It was a dingy-looking place with two windows, one on either side of the entrance. A rusty wire holder held a few newspapers, and there were a number of boards advertising various brands of cigarettes on the pavement in front of the shop and fastened to the shop-front itself. In the windows were piled a collection of tinned foods, cheap toys, lighters, cigarettes, and some rather sticky-looking sweets.

Leek opened the door and went into the dark interior. A jangling bell heralded his entrance, but it was some time before anyone came to attend to him. Presently, after what seemed to the waiting sergeant an incredibly long time, there was a shuffling sound from an archway at the back of the shop, and an old man appeared. He was a queer little fellow with a very bent back, wearing a skullcap that had originally been black but was now a rusty brown. His eyes, deeply sunk, were red-rimmed and watery, and his gnarled hands were crooked and shaking.

'Good afternoon,' he greeted in a quavering voice.

'I want a bottle of lemonade,' said Leek, seeing several bottles on a shelf behind the counter. 'I'd like to drink it here.'

He put down two shillings on the counter. The old man reached for a bottle and gave it to him. It had a screw top so that the sergeant was able to open it fairly easily.

'I s'pose you've had this shop for a long time?' said Leek as the old man fumbled in an ancient till for the change.

'Nearly fifty years. In the country, it were, when I first come. Changed a bit round these parts since then, it 'as.'

Leek swallowed some of his lemonade. It wasn't likely that he would get any information here, he thought, but there was no harm in trying. 'I expect it 'as. Turnin' it into quite a town, now, eh?'

The old man nodded. He seemed

pleased to talk to somebody. 'It's a big place ter what it used to be. All them new shops in the 'igh street, an' lots of new 'ouses. Oh yes, it's a big place now.'

'Well, I expect it's good for trade.'

'I don't do so well,' answered the old man sadly. 'The new people mostly go ter the big places for what they want, yer see. In the old days there wasn't more'n 'alf a dozen shops round 'ere. I don't know 'ow long I'll be here. The council is wantin' to pull the old shop down, yer see. Plannin' ter build flats.' He shook his head. 'Too much buildin', I say. There won't be a bit o' country left soon.'

'Yes,' agreed Leek, taking another swig at his lemonade, 'it seems a pity, but I s'pose it gives work to a lot o' people. O' course, there's those that suffer for all this 'ere expansion. There was that feller what 'ad his bungalow taken away from him, wasn't there? I s'pose you remember him?'

'I remember 'im, right enough,' exclaimed the man, and his watery eyes momentarily lost their weakness and looked angry. 'That was a wicked thing, that was. As nice a feller as could be, 'e was.'

'Did you know him?'

'Very well, I knew him. 'E used ter come in 'ere for cigarettes an' groceries. 'Is bungalow was only a step away from the shop, yer see. Many a chat we've 'ad. A nice lad, 'e was.'

The sergeant breathed a prayer of thankfulness. He had struck lucky. Almost by sheer accident, he had stumbled on someone who had known Penfold. Of course, the old shopkeeper might not have any fresh information to offer — but then again, he might.

'Used ter come in 'ere of a mornin',' continued the old man, 'an' buy 'is paper an' cigarettes. Wicked, it was, what they done to 'im.'

'Nice feller, was 'e?'

''E was,' replied the old man, nodding, 'though 'e'd bin through a lot o' 'ardship durin' the war. Goin' ter be married, too. Law or no law, it was a wicked thing they did — a wicked thing.'

''E didn't have to kill himself,' said Leek. 'That wasn't very sensible.'

'Maybe it weren't. But we've no right ter say whether it was or no. It weren't *our* 'ome what was taken, was it? 'E'd bin through a lot, yer see. This were the last straw.'

'He wasn't the only one who suffered in the war. There's many what 'ad a bad time.'

''E'd 'ad trouble before the war. More trouble than what the others 'ad, poor feller.'

Leek pricked up his ears. What *was* this trouble that Penfold had had before the war? Was his star in the ascendant, and was he about to learn something that *hadn't* come out before?

'Had a lot of trouble, had 'e?' he asked carelessly. 'Financial trouble or fam'ly trouble?'

'Fam'ly trouble, yer'd call it,' said the old man.

'Where was 'is family?' asked the sergeant, trying to control his mounting excitement. 'Why didn't they 'elp him? Surely they could've stopped him doin' what 'e did?'

The old man shook his head. Resting

136

his gnarled hands on the edge of the counter, he leaned forward. 'That was the thing, you see. He hadn't a family.'

'You mean they was all dead?'

'No, I don't mean nothin' of the kind. I don't know why 'e should've told *me* about it. It seems 'e'd kept it a kind of secret most of his life. But 'e told *me* — one mornin' when he'd come in to buy 'is paper. It was somethin' in the paper, I think, what started 'im talkin'.'

The old shopkeeper paused to get his breath. Leek waited expectantly.

''E asked me not to say anythin', an' I never 'ave,' went on the old man. 'But I don't s'pose it matters very much now. He's dead, poor feller, an' nobody can't do him any more 'arm. Yer see, his name weren't Penfold.' He brought out his information triumphantly, hoping to achieve his sensation. He had kept his knowledge to himself until the desire for infusing a little excitement into his drab life had got the better of his caution. Why he should have chosen Leek as his confidant, in preference to any of his other customers, was something known only to himself. Probably because the sergeant was a stranger, or perhaps because he was lonely and wanted to interest his customer so that he would stay a while. Whatever his reason, Leek thanked his stars that fate had sent him to this dingy little shop that afternoon.

'What was his name, then?' he asked.

The old man shook his head. 'I can't tell yer that. 'E didn't tell me what it was, only that it weren't Penfold.'

'Seems a queer thing. Why did 'e call himself Penfold, if it wasn't his name?'

'Ah, that was the trouble, yer see. 'E did tell me *that*. It was on account of 'is father.'

'What did his father do?'

''E was only a boy when it 'appened. Sixteen 'e was, poor feller. 'Is father killed his mother, yer see. Strangled 'er, he did.'

What the sergeant had expected, he couldn't have said. But it was certainly not *this*. He had made a discovery with a vengeance. He could almost see Mr. Budd's face when he told him. 'Nasty thing to 'ave happened,' he said. 'Nasty for the boy, I mean. His father was hanged, I suppose?'

'No, 'e wasn't,' said the old man. ''E was found guilty, but they said 'e was insane. 'E was shut up in that place — what do they call it?'

'Broadmoor?' suggested the sergeant.

'That's right,' said the old man, nodding. 'That's the place. So yer see, 'e changed his name because 'e didn't want people ter know that he was the son of a murderer what was shut up in this mad 'ouse.'

'He seems to have had a pretty bad time all round,' said Leek. 'Is his father still alive?'

But the old man could supply no further information. He seemed to regret his garrulousness, for he suddenly became quite taciturn.

Leek bought some milk chocolate and took his departure, happier than he had been when he arrived. It had been the greatest bit of luck. He could scarcely wait to get back to the Yard and make his report to Mr. Budd.

★　★　★

That individual, unaware of the sensational news that the sergeant was hurrying to bring him, was pondering over the item of information he had just learned from Mr. Grindthorpe.

So it had been Humphrey Gamble who had sold the land to the unfortunate Penfold. That definitely supplied a link between the two murdered men and the Penfold tragedy. It looked as if there might be a motive here for the murders. From what the solicitor had been able to tell him, it appeared that Gamble had been in the habit of buying land, when the opportunity came his way, to resell at a profit. The deal he had made with Richard Penfold had been quite a fair one. Humphrey Gamble's profit had not amounted to more than twenty percent. Not by any stretch of the imagination could he be blamed for what had happened subsequently. But to the warped mind of the red tape killer — and he certainly *had* a warped mind, whoever he was, or he wouldn't have chosen the method he had — Gamble's connection with the Penfold affair might have been sufficient to put him among those responsible.

After Mr. Grindthorpe had gone, the superintendent collected some more tea and toast and sat for some considerable time, munching and cogitating. By the time he left the teashop, he concluded that Timothy Smithson would have got back to his office, and he decided to pay him a visit.

Miss Catkin received him in a flutter of excitement. She had read in her favourite morning paper of the murder of Charles Gilmore, and had been pleasurably thrilled. 'It's really awful, it is really,' she said. 'First poor Mr. Humphrey and now this other man. One doesn't feel safe, you know. Do you think there'll be any more?'

'I couldn't say, miss,' answered Mr. Budd truthfully. 'Is Mr. Smithson in?'

'Oh, yes. He's in the inner office, now, you know. Mr. Gamble left him everything, the business and all the money. Of course, the will has to come up for probate, but in the meanwhile, Mr. Smithson is carrying on the business.'

There was, thought Mr. Budd, the slightest trace of resentment in Miss Catkin's voice. Perhaps she didn't *quite* approve of the managing clerk's promotion from the outer to the inner office. Nevertheless, she showed Mr. Budd in with the perfect decorum of a good secretary.

Timothy Smithson sat in the chair of his late employer, frowning at a document that lay on the blotting-pad before him. The office was still dusty and dingy. There had, it was true, been little time to make any improvements, but Mr. Budd thought that however much time there was, there would be little change while the managing clerk was in charge. What had suited Humphrey Gamble would suit Timothy Smithson. Dinginess and dust had been almost part of his training.

'Sorry to disturb you, Mr. Smithson,' he said as the managing clerk looked up. 'There's somethin' that I'd like to ask you in connection with this affair.'

Timothy Smithson leaned back in his chair, took off his spectacles, and gently rubbed his eyes. 'Anything I can do to help, I shall, of course, be only too pleased to do.'

'Just over a year ago,' said Mr. Budd, 'a man named Richard Penfold committed suicide because 'is bungalow — '

'What has this got to do with your investigation?' interrupted Timothy Smithson. 'I understand you've been making inquiries of Mrs. Bristow, but — '

'She told you, did she?' said Mr. Budd, interrupting in his turn.

The managing clerk inclined his head. 'She told me. Mrs. Bristow is my stepsister.'

'I see. I s'pose you knew Richard Penfold?'

'I can't see the object of these questions, Superintendent,' said Timothy Smithson, frowning. 'I understood that you were investigating these murders, not an unfortunate man who committed suicide over a year ago.'

'I *am* investigating the murders, sir. It's my opinion that there may be a connection.'

The managing clerk raised his eyebrows. 'A connection? How could there be?'

'Are you aware that Mr. Gamble sold the land to Penfold on which he built his bungalow?'

Timothy Smithson looked surprised. 'Yes, of course. I was instrumental in arranging the deal. What has *that* got to do with it?'

'It has this to do with it, sir. Mr. Gamble sold the land to Penfold, and Mr. Gilmore acted for the council over the compulsory purchase. Both, you might say, was indirectly responsible for Penfold's death.'

'Nonsense. Neither of them had anything to do with it. The only person responsible for Penfold's death was Penfold himself.'

'There might be somebody who didn't look at it like that.'

The managing clerk pursed his thin lips and gently stroked his chin with the tips of his fingers. 'It appears to me to be a very far-fetched idea. Even supposing it to be — er — probable, who is there who would be likely to resort to such extremes for the sake of — er — private vengeance?'

'I was hoping that you'd be able to help us there.'

'How can *I* help you? I've no idea. I believe you're wasting your time following up this line of inquiry, Superintendent. There's absolutely no one sufficiently interested in poor Penfold to go about murdering people whose responsibility for his death is problematical. If there were . . . ' He smiled without mirth, ' . . . I myself might be in danger.'

'Because you helped to put the deal through?'

'Exactly.' Timothy Smithson took out his handkerchief and began to polish his glasses carefully. 'No, no. Penfold's death has nothing to do with these terrible murders. This man is a maniac, Superintendent. There can be no reasonable motive for these killings.'

'I hope you're wrong, sir,' said Mr. Budd gravely. 'So you can't suggest anyone close enough to Penfold who might have a sufficiently strong grudge against these two people to wish to kill 'em?'

'There isn't such a person,' asserted the

managing clerk, shaking his head. 'Penfold hadn't any relations, and I can assure you that the Bristows don't bear any deep feeling of — er — anger against anybody.'

'You don't consider that Penfold was badly treated, sir?'

'It was very unfortunate,' said Timothy Smithson cautiously. 'But these things happen, you know. The law doesn't always take into account the — er — feelings of individuals. It would be next to impossible to do so. The — er — council, in the Penfold case, certainly did not err on the side of generosity, but their hands were tied to a certain extent. They acted entirely within their rights. There was nothing to do but accept the fact and make the best of it.'

The superintendent wondered if Timothy Smithson would have accepted the fact if it had happened to him. He decided that he probably would. There was nothing more to be learned from him, and Mr. Budd took his leave, refusing the cup of tea which Miss Catkin brought in just as he was going, to her obvious disappointment.

Mr. Budd made his way back to the Yard. He had a lot to think about. Very soon, he was to have a great deal more.

* * *

Timothy Smithson drank the tea Miss Catkin brought him and nibbled at one of the digestive biscuits which, following his late employer's custom, he now had with it.

Throughout his long and uneventful life, he had always wished to have his own legal practice. He had passed all the examinations, but lack of money had kept him working for somebody else. Now, at last, through the generosity of Mr. Gamble, it seemed he had achieved his desire.

Sitting back in his chair behind the writing-table, he let his eyes travel slowly round the dingy office. It was his now. Miss Catkin brought *him* tea at precisely four o'clock each afternoon, as she'd once brought it to Mr. Gamble. The business was entirely under his control. He was his own master.

And yet, he thought with a sigh, it didn't seem so wonderful as it would once have done. The thrill was already wearing off, even after so short a time. The feeling of responsibility crowded in on him sometimes — like now, as he sat there alone, nibbling at his biscuit. He had to make the decisions. There was nobody to consult, as there had been.

He was getting old, that was the trouble. Old and tired. With most of his life behind him, there wasn't much he could look forward to. He had become set in his habits. This unusual prosperity could bring him little; only care and responsibility.

Why, he thought, did things always happen *too late*? Twenty years earlier, he would have rejoiced in his new position. He would have tackled it with energy and enthusiasm. But now, he felt it was a burden that weighed heavily on his stooping shoulders. Perhaps he would be wise later to seek a partner, a younger man, or even sell the business. But that would mean that he would have nothing to occupy his time. He had never had any hobbies. His profession had always provided him with all the interests he needed.

There had been a time in his younger days — his very much younger days — when he had contemplated being a barrister, of appearing in court and pleading lost causes, and winning. But this ambition had been denied him, again from lack of money. He could not afford to set himself up in chambers and wait for the briefs to come in. He had to earn a living — a job that brought in a weekly wage. Well, he hadn't got to bother about that anymore; but the zest had gone — lost in those dusty years.

Timothy Smithson sighed again and passed a hand wearily over his forehead. Perhaps, he thought, the saddest words in the language were 'too late'.

At half-past five, Miss Catkin came in with the letters for him to sign. 'If there's nothing else,' she said, 'I should like to go. I want to catch the shops before they close.'

'Yes, yes, of course, Miss Catkin,' said Timothy Smithson. He realised as he said it that she would never have made a similar request to Humphrey Gamble. It irritated him a little that she should treat him any differently, but he made no comment. He signed the letters, and she gathered them up to put them in their envelopes and take them to the post.

'I'll say good night, then,' she said.

'Good night, Miss Catkin,' he answered, and she went out. In a few minutes he heard the door of the outer office open and close. She had gone.

Timothy Smithson turned his attention to the document he had been reading when Mr. Budd had interrupted him earlier, but he found that he could not concentrate on it. He read two of the clauses in it without taking in their meaning, and pushed it aside.

He felt restless. The dingy office was getting on his nerves this evening. There was no reason, except force of long habit, why he should stay there. But he waited until six o'clock, his usual time for leaving, before he put on his hat and shabby overcoat, locked up the office, and set off for home.

He lived in a furnished bed-sitting room in Bloomsbury. He had lived there for over fifteen years now. His landlady provided him with breakfast and an evening meal and full board at the weekends. It wasn't a very luxurious room, but it suited old Timothy Smithson's simple wants, and it wasn't expensive, which had always been a consideration.

It was his habit to go out for a short walk after his evening meal, choosing the less frequented streets and the squares which abound in that district of London. Wet or fine, snow or storm, Timothy Smithson invariably took his half-hour constitutional.

He did so that evening. His landlady was in the hall when he went out, and she exchanged a few remarks with her lodger about the state of the weather. She never heard him come back, but she didn't worry, thinking that she must have missed the sound of his key in the lock.

★   ★   ★

A patrolling policeman found him. He was lying by the railings of the central garden on the north side of Brunswick Square.

He was dead, and the tightly knotted piece of red tape round his throat left no doubt as to how his death had been brought about . . .

*   *   *

In the corner of an obscure teashop, a small notebook lay open on the stained table. A hand holding a cheap ballpoint pen hovered over the page, which contained a short list of names.

Two of them had already been crossed out in red.

The hand holding the pen firmly drew a line through the third name . . .

9

It was due to Sergeant Leek that Mr. Budd was still at Scotland Yard when the news of the third red tape murder came through.

The superintendent had found the sergeant waiting for him when he returned after his visit to Timothy Smithson, and almost bursting with a desire to impart his news. Mr. Budd listened while his subordinate related the result of his visit to the little shop in Stonehurst Green, enlarging, from a vivid imagination, on his own perspicacity in finding it.

'You can cut out tellin' me how clever you've been,' said Mr. Budd, breaking into a long and eulogistic account of the sergeant's remarkable genius. 'You've done very well, but it was mostly luck.'

'Nobody else could've done it,' declared Leek. 'It's a gift, that's what it is. You've either got it, or you 'aven't got it — '

'An' you've got it,' interrupted Mr. Budd. 'All right — you've got it! It's a pity you don't use it more often, but we'll be thankful for small mercies. Now that we've got this bit of information, we've got to decide what we're goin' to do next.'

'I thought I might 'ave a day off,' suggested Leek hopefully. 'It's been a pretty 'eavy mental strain.'

'The only time you're not under a mental strain is when you're asleep. So it isn't often you're subjected to one! This is the first real day's work you've done in about eighteen months. I s'pose it'll take you another year to recover from it?'

'Only a day.'

'Well, you're not gettin' a day,' snapped Mr. Budd. 'I don't know how you've got the nerve to ask for such a thing. We've got a lot o' work to do.'

'Well, you could be gettin' on with somethin',' said Leek brightly.

'Thank you, that's very kind of you. I s'pose I could do all the work while you snored away in yer bed an' forgot there was such a thing as crime an' criminals, eh? Maybe you'd like to stop there altogether, an' I could bring you yer pay packet every week? Or p'raps that might disturb you?'

'There's no need to be sarcastic,' answered the sergeant in an injured voice. 'You can't say I 'aven't been useful. I've got hold of an important bit of information.'

'I'm givin' you full credit for it. It may prove to be the clue we're searchin' for.'

The sergeant looked pleased.

'Somethin' told me, when I saw that shop, that it was the right place,' he remarked untruthfully. 'A queer sort o' feelin' came over me.'

'Indigestion, I expect. A kind of workin' colic. Now, let's get down to business! Penfold's father was put in Broadmoor because he strangled his wife. Accordin' to this old shopkeeper, Penfold was sixteen at the time. Hm. He was thirty-eight when he shot himself.'

''Ow do you know that?' asked Leek.

'I read it in the paper. It was mentioned at the inquest. Now that'd make it . . . let me see . . . twenty-two years ago that his father was put in Broadmoor.' He frowned. 'Twenty-two years ago,' he continued after a pause. 'Is he *still* there, I wonder, or is he dead?'

'He might've been released. They *do* release 'em, sometimes.'

'I was thinkin' that,' remarked Mr. Budd, staring up at the ceiling. 'An' he was a strangler, eh — ? We've got to find out what his name was, an' all about him.'

'Do you believe 'e could be the red tape feller?'

'I don't believe anythin',' said Mr. Budd rather extravagantly. 'But I'd like to know just *where* Penfold's father is today.' He pulled the house telephone towards him and asked to be put through to the C.R.O. 'Hello,' he said when he was connected. 'I want to speak to Inspector Whayles. This is Sup'n'tendent Budd. All right, I'll hang on.'

After a few minutes, Whayles came on the line. 'Hello,' he said. 'What can we do for you? A good line of fingerprints? Or we have some excellent photographs suitable for hanging in the children's nursery. Take your choice. Murders, bank robbers, con men.'

'I'll have a murderer, if you can find 'im,' said Mr. Budd.

'If he's ever been convicted, we'll find him.'

'Don't you be too sure,' grunted Mr. Budd. 'This feller was convicted of stranglin' his wife, an' sent to Broad-moor.'

'What's his name?'

'That's just what I can't tell yer. That's what I what *you to* tell *me*.'

'What's the catch? I'll buy it.'

'There's no catch. I'm lookin' for the name of a man what killed his wife by stranglin' her, about twenty-two years ago.'

'That'ud be in nineteen thirty-eight.'

'Round about that time. Though I wouldn't be certain to a year, or maybe two. I can tell you one thing that may help — this feller had a son who was about fifteen or sixteen.'

'It all seems to be 'about' or 'around' or 'somewhere near',' said Inspector Whay-les. 'All right, I'll do my best.'

'There can't be so many men who strangled their wives an' got sent to Broadmoor, so you ought to be able to tackle it.'

'We'll tackle anything,' said Whayles cheerfully. 'Don't worry, I'll find this feller for you.'

He rang off, and Mr. Budd hung up the receiver and leaned back in his chair. 'Well,' he remarked, fishing one of his black cigars out of his waistcoat pocket and sniffing at it, 'that's started the ball rolling.'

'I wonder if this feller *is* still in Broadmoor?' said Leek, eying the cigar apprehensively. The acrid smoke always irritated his throat and made him cough. 'If 'e is, it isn't goin' ter help much.'

'He may be still in Broadmoor, he may be dead, or he may be runnin' around stranglin' lawyers with red tape. There's no tellin' yet. I wonder why Penfold told this old chap you saw.'

'I dunno,' said the sergeant, shaking his head.

'It seems a bit queer that after takin' so much trouble to keep it to himself,' went on Mr. Budd thoughtfully, 'that he should've opened up his heart to an old man keepin' a shop. I could understand it if he'd told the Bristows, or even Lucy Bristow.' He stuck the cigar in his mouth and felt in his pocket for his matches. 'It strikes me as peculiar.'

'It might've just come over him,' said Leek. 'Yer can't tell why people do thin's. Sort of impulse, I expect.'

To his surprise, the superintendent didn't argue. Instead he nodded slowly, struck a match and lighted the cigar carefully.

Sergeant Leek, perched on the edge of his chair, watched the wreaths of pungent smoke as they drifted across the office. He would have liked to go home, but he dared not make the suggestion. His attempt to get a day off had met with such a withering refusal that he wasn't going to risk another.

Mr. Budd, wedged in his desk chair, seemed to have settled there permanently. With half-closed eyes, he puffed at his cigar, the picture of sleepy enjoyment. But Leek, who knew him better than anybody, was not deceived. Behind that drowsy mask a keen brain was busy. It was during these apparently lazy periods that Mr. Budd marshalled all the information at his disposal and evolved his theories.

He was a confirmed believer that physical effort detracted from mental concentration. The brain required all the energy it could extract from the body if it was to function at the height of its power. Any physical exercise drew away a portion of this energy — the greater the exercise, the larger the portion — and the brain functioned less efficiently. This was at the bottom of the stout man's apparent laziness. He was, in point of fact, an extremely energetic man, but it was a mental energy, not a physical one. In this respect, he differed from Leek, who suffered from both physical and mental inertia.

Presently, the buzz of the house telephone roused Mr. Budd from his thoughts. Hoisting himself forward in his chair, he stretched out an arm and lifted the receiver from its rest. The voice of

Inspector Whayles sounded in his ear.

'I've found your man,' he said. 'Chap named Herbert Renshaw. Killed his wife, Elizabeth, on Sunday, December the second, nineteen hundred and thirty-seven. Strangled her with a silk stocking. Was found insane and sent to Broadmoor.'

'That sounds like the feller,' said Mr. Budd.

'There was no other murder by strangulation around the period you mentioned. And no murderer was sent to Broadmoor.'

'Which seems to make it pretty certain,' grunted Mr. Budd. 'Where is Renshaw now?'

'I was keeping that tit-bit for you. He escaped from Broadmoor eighteen months ago.'

'Escaped, did he?' exclaimed Mr. Budd. 'Did they recapture 'im?'

'No, he's still at large. Looks as if you might be on to something. It's this red tape business, isn't it?'

'That's right. Have you got Renshaw's full record?'

'We've got everything. This is the most efficient department in the Yard. Didn't you know?'

'I'll take your word for it. Can you send along everythin' you've got about Renshaw to my office?'

'Be with you in five minutes,' promised Whayles.

He was better than his word. It was barely three minutes later that a messenger arrived with a bulky folder. Mr. Budd signed the printed chit for it, opened the folder, and prepared to study the contents.

Shorn of the official language, Renshaw's story was a fairly simple one. Up to the time of the murder he had been a quiet, well-behaved man devoted to his family, which had consisted of his wife and young son. For some years he had had a job with a firm of radio manufacturers as manager of the dispatch department, and then gradually a change had come over him. He had developed fits of depression and irritability. He suffered from lapses of memory. His work began to deteriorate, and eventually became so bad that he got the sack.

He had found it difficult to get another job, and this had preyed on his mind. Anxiety for the future had apparently reached a climax on the night of the murder. His son, a boy of fourteen, was spending the weekend with an aunt, otherwise he might have shared the same fate as his mother. Renshaw had made no secret of what he had done. Distraught, and in a dazed condition, he had telephoned the police station in the early hours of Sunday morning, stating that he had strangled his wife. The reason he gave, when they came, was that the utter hopelessness of the future had suddenly overwhelmed him. He had killed her to save her from suffering the effects of poverty. The verdict at the trial had been the only possible one — guilty but insane.

That was the simple, and rather pathetic, story of Herbert Renshaw. Some queer kind of bug had got into his brain and slowly destroyed the balance of his mind. From a normal, quite ordinary man, he had developed into a murderer.

Mr. Budd looked at the police photographs. He saw an inoffensive, rather nondescript-looking man — the kind of man who could be seen in thousands, any day during the rush hour, on Tubes and buses and trains. The eyes were set a little close to the short nose, and the chin was weak, the hair receded slightly from the narrow forehead. The big man slowly read the description: *Height: 5 ft. 9 inches. Hair: Brown, turning grey at temples. Colour of eyes: Pale blue. Complexion: Sallow. Build: Slight. Distinguishing marks: Large mole on inner side of right thigh. Vaccination marks on upper right arm, unusually large and well-marked. Voice: Low, but apt to rise under excitement or emotional strain. Age: 52.* Underneath, in red ink, had been added the inscription: '*This man escaped from Broadmoor on October the 12th, 1958 and is still at large.*'

'And is still at large,' repeated Mr. Budd to himself.

Leek had wandered over and was standing behind his superior's chair, looking over his broad shoulder. 'Don't think we need ter look any further,' he remarked.

'What d'you mean?' grunted Mr. Budd.

'Renshaw's the feller we want,' explained the sergeant. 'It all fits.'

'Maybe it does. But I don't know what you mean by not needin' to look any further. Do *you* know where to find Renshaw?'

'No, of course I don't.'

'No more does anyone else. They've bin lookin' for him since October the twelfth, nineteen fifty-eight, an' they haven't found him.'

'He must be somewhere.'

'That's a brilliant remark, that is,' snarled Mr. Budd scathingly. 'Of course he's somewhere. The question is — where? Don't breathe down the back of my neck!'

'Sorry. We've got ter find 'im somehow, haven't we?'

Mr. Budd admitted the truth of this. 'But I don't know how,' he added, shaking his head. 'The whole of the police force in the country's been lookin' for him ever since he escaped. They're still lookin'. An' I'll bet every line of investigation has been tried. What more can *we* do?'

'I'll give me mind to it.'

Mr. Budd regarded the complacent expression on the sergeant's face malignantly. 'The thing that's so engagin' about you,' he said, 'is yer modesty.'

'I was never given to blowin' me own trumpet,' said Leek with satisfaction. 'But you'd be surprised what I'm capable of.'

'I wouldn't be surprised at anythin' concernin' you. I s'pose you was born like it.'

'I don't know where I get it from. It's me unconscious mind workin'.'

'Well, it's got plenty of time. Your conscious mind never does any.'

'A sort of inspiration wells up inside me,' went on Leek, ignoring the interruption. 'It's the queerest thin'.'

'If it's got anythin' to do with you, it must be. Now, just stop talkin' a lot o' rubbish an' let me think, will you?'

The sergeant sighed. 'I'm only tryin' to 'elp,' he said dolefully. 'After all, if it hadn't been for me, you'd never have got on to Renshaw at all, would yer?'

'That's true. Yes, I'll give you credit for that. Maybe the same kind of luck 'ull help us find out where Renshaw is now.'

Leek marched over to his chair and sat down. 'How did this feller manage to escape?' he asked.

'He just walked out. Coshed the postman, changed into his clothes, an' walked out. Easy as kiss yer hand.'

'I s'pose they've got in touch with this 'aunt' the boy went to stay with?' said Leek, rubbing his forehead.

'They're sure to. An' any other relatives as well.' He got ponderously to his feet. 'I'm goin' to find out who's in charge of this Renshaw business. I expect it'll mean a visit to Berkshire.'

He left the office, and Leek settled himself in his chair as comfortably as he could. He felt that he had done a good day's work, and was looking forward to the time when he could go home. But there were no fixed hours at Scotland Yard, nor any extra pay for overtime. When you were on a job you kept on, snatching what time you could for rest and meals, until it was completed. The next best thing to going home was to try and put one over on Mr. Budd. If he could only think of some way to find out where Renshaw was. That would be a feather in his cap. Not only would he put one over on the superintendent, but on the rest of the police force as well.

But it wasn't so easy. Rack his brains as he would, he could think of nothing. He had just fallen into a doze when Mr. Budd came back.

'I'm goin' to Berkshire in the mornin',' he announced wearily, 'to see the governor of Broadmoor. Blenkiron's got the job in hand here, but there's precious little information. When Renshaw walked out in his postman rig, he seems to've walked off the earth. There's been no trace of him since.'

'How's the governor of Broadmoor goin' to 'elp?' asked Leek.

'I don't know,' confessed Mr. Budd, yawning, 'but it's as good a startin'-off place as any. I think we may as well be gettin' home. I want to make an early start in the mornin'.'

It was at that moment that the news of Timothy Smithson's murder reached him.

★ ★ ★

The wind cutting across the central garden in Brunswick Square was cold, and a thin drizzle of rain had begun to fall, but the unpleasantness of the night did not prevent the usual crowd from gathering as soon as the news leaked out that a murder had been committed. People of all kinds and descriptions materialised from apparently nowhere, pressing eagerly forward round the roped-off place by the railings where the body of Timothy Smithson lay.

Inside the enclosure, a group of people consisting of the divisional surgeon, a detective-superintendent, the official photographers, and several uniformed constables went methodically about the job that had brought them there.

'Sup'n'tendent Budd 'ull be here in a few minutes,' said the superintendent.

'Better leave everything until he arrives.'

Almost as he spoke, a police car drew up on the outskirts of the little crowd, and Mr. Budd, followed by Sergeant Leek, got heavily out. He forced his way through the curious sightseers and ducked with difficulty under the rope. After a few words with the superintendent, he went over and peered down at the dead man. The latest victim of the red tape murderer had not as yet been identified. Only the notification of the discovery and the method of murder had been telephoned to the Yard, and it was with something of a shock that Mr. Budd, in spite of the congested and swollen features, recognised Timothy Smithson.

'Hm,' he grunted. 'He didn't 'ave much time to enjoy his inheritance, did he?'

'Do you know the man?' asked the superintendent.

The big man nodded. 'Yes. His name's Timothy Smithson, an' he was managing clerk to Humphrey Gamble.'

'The first chap to be killed by this red tape maniac.'

'That's right. Well, we'd better get on with the job. Have yer photographed him yet?'

The superintendent shook his head. 'Waited for you,' he said laconically.

Mr. Budd turned to the police photographer. 'Do your stuff,' he ordered curtly.

The photographer 'did his stuff'. The flashes of bulbs lit up the scene with blinding intensity as several pictures were taken from various angles suggested by Mr. Budd. When this had been done, the divisional surgeon, who had been waiting impatiently, came forward and made his examination.

'Death was due to asphyxia,' he said, looking up, after a brief examination of the body. 'The asphyxia was caused by a constriction of the windpipe due to a piece of thin red tape having been tied tightly round the throat.'

'In other words, he was strangled,' said Mr. Budd. 'All right, Doctor. Let me 'ave a report after the post-mortem, will you? We'll see what there is in the pockets, an' then the body can be removed.'

With the assistance of the superintendent, he knelt down and rapidly went through the dead man's pockets. There wasn't much in any of them. A little money in silver and copper, a worn wallet containing two pound notes and a ten-shilling note, a bunch of keys, and two bills, one for newspapers and one for laundry.

'This must be his address,' muttered Mr. Budd, looking at them. 'He lived quite close, apparently. We'll go round there in a minute.' He got up and brushed the damp knees of his trousers. 'Better make a search of the vicinity, I s'pose, just in case there's anythin' the murderer may have left. There won't be anythin', but we'd better make sure.'

It was one of the constables who made the discovery. 'There's somethin' 'ere, sir,' he said, peering through the railings of the central garden. 'Look, yer can see it — in that bit of grass.'

Mr. Budd came quickly to his side. Close to the railing, half-concealed by the long grass, lay a glass object. 'This is somethin' in your line, Doctor,' he said, turning to the police surgeon. 'It's a hypodermic syringe, isn't it?'

The doctor joined him and, bending down, looked at the place where Mr. Budd pointed. 'It certainly looks like one.'

'We've got to get hold of it,' said Mr. Budd. 'Be careful how you handle it, though. It may bear prints.'

'I'll get it, sir,' volunteered the policeman who had first seen it. He climbed over the railings and approached the spot where the little object lay.

'Pick it up by the needle,' said the doctor.

The constable did so, and passed it gingerly through the railings to Mr. Budd. The superintendent took it carefully. 'Get a box out of the bag,' he said to Leek, and the sergeant made his way to the place where Mr. Budd had deposited the murder bag, which was carried by every detective engaged on a murder inquiry, and contained an assortment of things likely to be of use in the preliminary investigation. Leek brought back a small cardboard box of a size that would contain the syringe. It was quite small, and still contained a tiny quantity of a colourless liquid.

'This is an important discovery,' remarked Mr. Budd, carefully depositing the syringe in the box. 'You might have a look on the body, Doctor, when you do the post-mortem, an' see if there's a puncture that might've been made by this thing.'

'You think he was drugged before he was strangled?' asked the doctor.

'It wouldn't surprise me. I've been wonderin' how the killer was able to overpower these fellers while he strangled 'em. There was no sign of any of 'em havin' been coshed, or anythin' of that sort.'

'Were any puncture marks found on the others?' asked the doctor.

'Nobody looked. They wouldn't be easy to find, would they? Not unless you was specially lookin' for 'em.'

The doctor agreed.

'I'll have this thing tested for prints,' said Mr. Budd, 'an' get the stuff in it analysed. I'll bet it's a pretty quick-workin' kind of dope of some sort.'

The doctor made a suggestion.

'Maybe that's the stuff,' said Mr. Budd. 'You'd know more about it than me. Put this back in the bag, will yer?' He handed the box with the syringe to Leek, and the sergeant put it away in the murder bag.

They continued the search, but there was nothing else. The ambulance arrived just as they finished, and the body was taken away to the mortuary.

'There's nothin' more to do here,' said Mr. Budd. 'We'll go along to the address on the paper bill.'

He left the superintendent and the policemen to deal with the dispersing crowd of sightseers, and was driven off with Leek in the police car that had brought them.

Timothy Smithson's landlady was shocked at the news of her lodger's death. 'Why, he only left here for his usual walk a little while ago,' she said. 'I spoke to him in the hall as he went out.'

'Did he always go out for a walk in the evenin', ma'am?' asked Mr. Budd.

'Yes, always. It didn't matter what the weather was; Mr. Smithson always took his walk as soon as he'd finished his dinner.'

'What time was that?'

'Half-past eight.'

'Was it always the same time?'

'Yes, Mr. Smithson was most particular about times.'

So, thought Mr. Budd, anybody who knew the dead man's habits would have been pretty certain of meeting him soon after eight-thirty any evening. The murderer only had to follow him until there was a suitable opportunity. It would only have taken a few minutes. A jab with the syringe, the red tape tied tightly round the neck, and it was done.

Yes, it would have been easy. But for whom?

Renshaw, the man who had walked out of Broadmoor and disappeared? Or — someone else . . . ?

10

The governor of Broadmoor Asylum for the Criminally Insane looked across the desk in his comfortable office at the stout figure of Mr. Budd perched uncomfortably on the chair opposite him. It was a well-made chair, but it had never been intended for the heavy burden it now supported, and it creaked in protest at every movement that Mr. Budd made.

'Renshaw was an exemplary prisoner in every way,' said the governor, playing with a pencil on the blotting-pad while he spoke. 'That's why he was allowed a certain amount of latitude. He was quiet and courteous; took part in the theatrical productions, which the patients do among themselves from time to time ... in fact, almost completely normal in every way.'

'Except one,' remarked Mr. Budd.

The governor shook his head. 'There

was no sign of that. He showed no — er — inclination towards violence in any way while he was here. It was a shock to me when I heard how he had escaped.'

'Exactly how *did* he escape?'

'Well, it was in the morning. Renshaw liked to take a walk in the grounds before breakfast. As I said, he was allowed a certain amount of latitude; a number of the people here who are well-behaved get special facilities. The first we knew there was anything wrong was when Renshaw didn't turn up for breakfast. I sent out to look for him. There was no sign of him, but the postman was found under a bush in the shrubbery, unconscious from a heavy blow on the head. He was dressed only in his underclothes, and Renshaw's outer garments were found piled up beside him. Of course, we knew what had happened at once. We warned the gatekeeper, but he stated that the postman had already left. He hadn't bothered to take much notice of him, naturally.' The governor picked up the pencil and twiddled it in his fingers.

'The alarm was given immediately, but Renshaw wasn't found.'

'Did he have any visitors while he was here?'

The governor shook his head. 'No, nobody ever came to see him. It's always been a mystery to me what happened to him. He only had the postman's uniform, but no one had seen a postman in the neighbourhood.'

'Somebody may have been waiting with a change of clothin',' suggested Mr. Budd.

'That's what the police thought. But who?'

'There was an aunt. The boy, Renshaw's son, was stayin' with her at the time of the murder.'

'She's dead — she died several years ago. Of course, the son might have had something to do with it. I put up that suggestion to the police, but nobody knew what had happened to him. He'd vanished completely.'

Mr. Budd could have told him what had happened to Renshaw's son, but he didn't. That was something that might be an advantage to keep to himself.

There was nothing much more to be learned from the governor, and he took his leave. He called at the local police station and interviewed the inspector who had organised the search for the missing man. But he gained no further helpful information.

'The whole thing was a puzzle,' declared the inspector, scratching his grizzled head. 'We threw a cordon round the entire district within a few minutes of the alarm reaching us, but he must've got through it somehow — how, I don't know.'

Mr. Budd went back to London. The first place he visited were the offices of Gamble, Gamble, Chalkit and Gamble. Miss Catkin, fluttering about like a frightened hen, almost dragged him into the outer office.

'Oh, dear me,' she wailed, 'this is dreadful, really *dreadful*! First poor Mr. Humphrey, and now Mr. Smithson. I'm frightened out of my wits. Who will be the next?'

'I don't think you're in any danger,'

murmured Mr. Budd soothingly.

'I've told her that,' broke in the voice of Miss Emily Gamble. She had come out of the inner office while Mr. Budd had been speaking.

'Good afternoon, miss,' said Mr. Budd. 'So you've heard the news?'

'I telephoned Miss Gamble at once,' put in Miss Catkin. 'I didn't know what to do.'

'And Miss Gamble telephoned *me*,' said Mr. Grindthorpe, appearing at the door of the private office. 'This is a terrible thing — a great shock to all of us. Poor Smithson! Why should this maniac killer have chosen him, eh? I'm looking after things here for Miss Gamble, you know. Don't know whether Smithson left a will, yet. If not, we'll have to find the next of kin, eh?'

Would that turn out to be Mrs. Bristow? Mr. Budd thought, but he kept it to himself.

'I believe Mr. Smithson had some relatives somewhere,' said Emily Gamble, 'but I don't know where. It's very dreadful — all these murders. Surely the police are doing *something* about it?'

'We're doin' all we can, miss,' said Mr. Budd.

'Of course, of course,' broke in Mr. Grindthorpe. 'Can't do miracles, you know, Emily — eh, Superintendent? Difficult job. No motive to help, you see. Have you got any fresh information?'

'We're following up one or two lines, sir,' answered Mr. Budd cautiously. 'I can't say whether they'll lead us anywhere or not.'

'But in the meanwhile, this horrible man may kill a lot *more* people,' cried Miss Catkin, clasping her hands to her thin breast. 'Can't *anything* be done to stop him?'

'At the present stage, I'm afraid not,' said Mr. Budd. 'You see, we don't know who the next one'll be, if there *is* a next, so we can't warn 'em, or offer 'em protection.'

'All you can be certain of,' said Mr. Grindthorpe, 'is that the next victim will be a lawyer, eh?'

'We can't even be certain of that, sir,' said the superintendent, shaking his head.

'He might try somebody in a different profession. You can't tell.'

Mr. Grindthorpe pursed his lips. 'Shouldn't think that was likely. They've all been lawyers up to now, eh? The man must have a kind of *idée fixe* about them, eh? And the red tape — wouldn't apply to another profession, you know.'

'Oh, *do* let's stop talking about it,' implored Miss Catkin. 'It makes me go cold all over. I shall be simply terrified to go home.'

'I'm quite sure you have nothing to fear, nothing to fear at all, Miss Catkin,' said Mr. Grindthorpe. 'I hardly think that you're likely to be singled out for this — er — maniac's attention, eh?'

'Most unlikely,' agreed Emily Gamble. 'There doesn't seem any reason for me to remain here any longer. If you are kindly going to look after the business, Joseph, until we know what is happening to it, there's nothing I can do.'

'No, no, Emily,' said Mr. Grindthorpe. 'You go along home. I'll attend to all that's necessary, with, of course, the assistance of Miss Catkin. You'll be remaining at Wellington Park, I suppose, eh?'

'I don't know,' answered Emily Gamble uncertainly. 'I haven't had time to make up my mind. It's been such a shock. I shall probably stay, if I can afford it. My annuity isn't very large, you know.'

Mr. Grindthorpe clicked his teeth and shook his shining head. 'I thought that was rather unfair of your brother. You gave up most of your life looking after him, eh? He might have shown his appreciation in a more practical way.'

Emily Gamble smiled a trifle wanly. 'Humphrey was peculiar in many way. He hadn't a very great opinion of women in business. That's why, no doubt, he left everything to Mr. Smithson. Anyway, I could never have looked after the business. I'm not qualified.'

'You could have sold it, or taken someone in as a partner, eh?' said Mr. Grindthorpe. 'Kept Smithson on as managing clerk, perhaps? At least, he could have left you more than a small annuity.'

'It's not much good talking about that

now, is it?' said Emily Gamble wearily. 'I expect, in any case, the business will have to be sold now.'

'I'll let you know when we've sorted things out,' said Mr. Grindthorpe. 'There's rather a muddle here, you know. Bundles of old documents and dust, eh? More dust than documents, eh? Don't know how Gamble and Smithson could work in all that muck and chaos. Couldn't do it myself, eh?'

'Maybe you'd like the keys,' said Mr. Budd. 'That's what I came along for. We found 'em on the body.' He took the bunch of keys from his pocket and gave them to the cherubic lawyer.

'That's very kind of you, Superintendent,' he said. 'I shall need them, of course, before I can open the safe. I was wondering what we were going to do about that, you know.'

'I thought somebody might be,' said Mr. Budd. 'Well, I must be gettin' back to the Yard.'

'You'll let me know if there's any fresh news, eh?' said Mr. Grindthorpe.

'And do *please* try and catch this awful

man before he can do any more damage,' put in Miss Catkin fervently.

Mr. Budd promised to do his best and walked down the stairs with Emily Gamble.

'Do you think there's any chance of finding this — this dreadful murderer?' she asked in a low voice as he was going to wish her goodbye.

'We usually *do* find 'em, miss.'

'But this is rather *unusual*, isn't it? I mean, it might be anybody. There's no motive to help you.'

'We can't be certain of that at present. All we can say is that no motive has yet come to light.'

'Do you think there *might* be a motive?'

'We've got to take the possibility into consideration, miss.'

'I don't see how there could be, in my brother's case. There was no reason why anyone should wish to kill Humphrey — I'm quite sure of that.'

'Maybe you're right, maybe not,' said Mr. Budd noncommittally. 'It's difficult to be sure about anythin'. Our job is to follow up every line of inquiry until we strike the right one.'

Emily Gamble looked at him doubtfully. 'Surely that wastes quite a lot of time?'

'I'm afraid it does. But you see, we can't tell which is the right line an' which is the wrong, so we've got to follow 'em all.'

'I hope you're successful. Will you let me know as soon as — as you've found the right line?'

'Everybody'll know then, miss,' said the superintendent; and he made his way back to the Yard. In his office he found an impatient Peter Ashton waiting for him.

'Where have you been?' demanded the reporter. 'I've called here twice today. What have you been up to?'

Mr. Budd carefully hung up his hat and coat and sat down at his desk. 'In case you don't know, I'm investigatin' a series of murders.'

'Of course I know. That's why I'm here.'

'After information, or bringin' information?'

'Have you *got* any information?'

Mr. Budd produced a cigar from his waistcoat pocket and bit off the end. 'Maybe I have,' he said slowly. 'An' again, maybe I haven't.'

'Now don't get in one of your irritating moods. Have you got any farther with this business?'

Mr. Budd considered the question while he carefully lit his cigar. 'Well,' he said at last, puffing out a cloud of acrid smoke, 'I have, but it's not for publication.'

'I've got to print something soon. Old Sorbet's in danger of a stroke! Three murders, and all I've written is a lot of tripe.'

'That's what you usually write, ain't it? If I'm goin' to tell you anythin', you've got to keep it to yerself until I give you permission.'

'All right, all right,' broke in Peter impatiently. 'We went into all that the other day. What have you found out?'

With great deliberation, Mr. Budd told him what he had learned concerning Renshaw. Peter Ashton listened with growing excitement.

'This is wonderful!' he exclaimed when Mr. Budd had finished. 'There can't be much doubt that this chap Renshaw is the red tape killer.'

'Now, don't you go so fast,' said Mr. Budd, frowning at the glowing end of his cigar. 'It's no good jumpin' to conclusions like that.'

'Don't you think so?'

'There's a great difference between thinkin' somethin' an' bein' able to prove it. Why should Renshaw want to kill these people?'

'Because of his son,' answered Peter promptly. 'That's obvious.'

'Is it? I don't think it's so obvious as you try to make out. How did Renshaw know that Penfold was his son? You see, the boy changed his name. Renshaw was shut up in Broadmoor, an' he didn't have any visitors or receive any letters. How did he know that this feller Penfold, who shot himself, was any relation at all?'

'I see what you mean,' answered Peter thoughtfully. 'He must have found out somehow.'

'You're tryin' to twist facts to suit a preconceived theory,' said Mr. Budd severely. 'There's nothin' to show that he *did* know.'

'Look here,' interrupted Peter as an idea struck him. 'Renshaw escaped from Broadmoor eighteen months ago, didn't he?'

'About that.'

'Well, that was *before* Penfold shot himself,' said Peter triumphantly. 'They could have actually met. In fact, it could have been *Penfold* who was responsible for helping his father to escape. How's that?'

'It's all right, so far as it goes. The trouble is, it doesn't go far enough. There's not a tittle of evidence to show that anythin' of the kind happened.'

'Somebody helped Renshaw to escape. That's certain.'

'It's nothin' of the kind.'

'He left his clothes behind him when he put on the postman's uniform, didn't he? I suppose you'll admit that's a fact?' Mr. Budd nodded. 'And another fact,' went on the reporter, 'is that he walked out of

Broadmoor wearing the postman's uniform?' Again Mr. Budd nodded. 'The alarm was given soon after, and the district was searched for a man in a postman's uniform, but he wasn't found, was he? How far do you think he would have got *if he'd still been wearing that uniform*? But he got away — he vanished completely. Somebody must have been waiting with a change of clothes, probably in a car.'

'There is an alternative,' murmured Mr. Budd.

'What?'

'I'm not tellin' you that. It's just an idea of my own. I'd rather keep it ter myself.'

Peter Ashton looked at him suspiciously. 'You've got one of your hunches. You've just had one of those bright illuminating flashes, haven't you?'

Mr. Budd blew a stream of smoke towards the ceiling. 'Well, I *have* just thought of somethin'.'

'I knew it,' cried Peter. 'I could tell by that smug expression! I've seen it so many times. And I suppose you're going to tell me that you've solved the mystery, eh?'

'I'm not goin' ter tell you anythin' o' the kind,' retorted the superintendent calmly. 'If you're talkin' about these red tape murders, I'm no nearer solvin' 'em than you are.'

'If we could only find Renshaw,' muttered Peter.

'Ah,' said Mr. Budd, stubbing out the chewed end of his cigar in the ashtray. '*If* we could find him.'

'Can't I just give a hint that there might be a connection between the red tape murderer and the man who escaped from Broadmoor?' pleaded Peter. 'It 'ud give a kick to my next story.'

'You'll get a kick, right enough,' grunted Mr. Budd, 'if you so much as print one word about it! I'll have that rag you draw your pay from sued for obstructin' the course o' justice. I'll give you the story when I know it, but I won't have anythin' printed before, see?'

Before Peter could reply, Sergeant Leek entered the office carrying some papers in his hand. 'Report 'as come through from Camelford,' he said, putting the papers down in front of Mr. Budd. 'There's also a report of the post-mortem on Smithson, an' a note about Gamble an' Gilmore. Hello, Mr. Ashton, 'ow are you?'

'Frustrated,' said Peter, 'that's what I am.'

'I can give yer a cure for that,' said Leek hopefully. 'Just let me put yer to sleep. A suggestion under 'ypnotism 'ull be received by your subconscious, an' you'll feel calm an' relaxed.'

'You're not goin' to turn this office into a circus,' snapped Mr. Budd. 'You can cut all that rubbish out.'

'I think I'll just stay frustrated,' said Peter hastily. 'What have you got there? Anything fresh?'

Mr. Budd shook his head without raising his eyes from the reports he was reading.

'Well, I might as well be going back to the office,' said Peter. 'What I'm going to say to Sorbet, I don't know.'

'You can tell 'im that a sensational development is expected soon,' suggested Mr. Budd.

'Is it?'

Mr. Budd shrugged his shoulders. 'It could be. Anythin's possible.'

'Except getting any sense out of you,' retorted Peter Ashton, and he left the office in disgust.

'He's cross,' remarked the sergeant lugubriously.

'He'll get over it,' grunted Mr. Budd. 'Well, there's nothin' fresh from Camelford. Lucy Bristow can't add anythin' to what we already know. These other reports are a bit better. I asked 'em to have a look for syringe marks on the bodies of Gamble an' Gilmore, as well as Smithson. They've found 'em. That means that all three of 'em was jabbed with a hypodermic syringe before they was strangled. The stuff in the syringe, we found, is a very powerful drug that 'ud take effect almost at once.'

'Where does that get us?'

'It don't get us anywhere, but it's a fact worth rememberin'.' Mr. Budd yawned. 'I'm goin' to call it a day. I'm goin' home to think.'

'That's a good idea,' said Leek, his long face brightening.

'You can stay 'ere in case any news comes through,' said his superior, putting on his overcoat. 'If it's anythin' important, you can phone me.'

The brightness fled from Leek's face. 'I could do with a bit of a rest meself,' he said. 'I feel worn out.'

'Just suggest to yer subconscious that you're full of energy an' enthusiasm, an' you'll feel fine,' said Mr. Budd, and he left the office.

*   *   *

In the bedroom of his neat little villa at Streatham, Mr. Budd lay on the bed, his head supported by several cushions from the sitting-room. It was dark outside, but he had not switched on the lamp. Only the glow of the electric fire illumined the room, which was hazy with smoke from the black cigar that was clenched between his teeth.

He was fully dressed except for his tie, which he had removed, and opened his shirt collar. He had come straight up to his bedroom after his evening meal for one of those periods of intense thinking that usually brought results. As a precaution against being disturbed by his housekeeper, who strongly disapproved of smoking in the bedroom, and her employer's habits in general, he had locked the door.

Tomorrow morning he would have to face the assistant commissioner with a report of his progress up to date, and he wasn't happy about it. Colonel Blair would expect results, and there weren't any. The superintendent was not afraid of a reprimand, but his reputation was excellent and he wanted to keep it that way. It was true that it was a difficult problem, and he hadn't as yet had very much time on it. All that could be done he had done, but he wasn't making enough headway to please himself. Perhaps, if he really thought over all the facts that had come into his possession, he could arrange them to make some sort of a pattern, even if it were only a vague one.

First of all, there was the murder of Humphrey Gamble. On his way home from the station at Wellington Park, he had been attacked by a person unknown, rendered unconscious by the injection of a drug from a hypodermic syringe, strangled with a piece of red tape, and, either afterwards or before, his body had been dragged under a clump of bushes on the waste ground near the spot where he had first been attacked. There was no obvious motive for the murder.

Secondly, there was the murder of Charles Gilmore under similar circumstances. On his way home from a meeting of the borough council in the Town Hall at Stonehurst Green, he had been attacked in the shadow of some trees in the public gardens. He also had first been rendered unconscious by the drug and then strangled by a length of red tape. Again no obvious motive.

Thirdly, there was the murder of Timothy Smithson. The same circumstances repeated. Still no definable motive.

There was, however, a nebulous link connecting all three victims of the red tape killer. Richard Penfold, the man who had shot himself because he was going to lose the bungalow he had built, under a compulsory purchase order of the council. Humphrey Gamble had sold him the land on which it had been built, while Timothy Smithson had assisted in putting the deal through — and he was also related to the mother of the woman to whom Penfold had been engaged. Charles Gilmore had acted as solicitor for the council in the matter of the compulsory purchase order. It was not a very tangible connection, but it *was* a connection.

So far, thought Mr. Budd, they had a pattern of a sort. These people had all been remotely mixed up in the Penfold affair. Therefore the Penfold affair *could* provide a motive for the murders. *If* someone had been sufficiently interested in Penfold to wish to seek vengeance for what had happened to him. The red tape used by the murderer fitted in with this theory, for in a way Penfold had been the victim of red tape.

But surely there were people more responsible than Gamble, Gilmore, and Smithson? There were, for instance, the actual members of the borough council. They had been a great deal more to blame. And apart from this, who *was* there sufficiently interested in Richard Penfold to commit cold-blooded murder in order to avenge his death?

There were the Bristows — and his father, Herbert Renshaw. Renshaw was the most likely. He had already used strangulation as a means of murder. But he hadn't *known* that Penfold was his son. Or had he?

Just for the sake of argument, thought Mr. Budd, supposing he had discovered that Richard Penfold was his son. Where did that lead?

Not very far. Renshaw had escaped from Broadmoor six months *before* Penfold had shot himself. Well, that was all right. They might have met during that six months and discovered the relationship between them. Penfold, even if he'd wished to, couldn't have mentioned anything about his father to anybody, in the circumstances. And having changed his name, and kept the relationship a secret for so long, it was unlikely that he *would* have wished to, in any case. But just supposing they had met and agreed to keep each other's secret — what then?

Well, then you came up against a thundering big snag. Why had Renshaw waited over a year before starting on his campaign of vengeance? Waiting to choose his victims? No, that didn't make sense. If he'd known the real identity of Penfold, he would have followed the proceedings that led to his death. There must be another reason.

Could it be that Renshaw had not been in a position to carry out his plan of vengeance during that twelve-month period? That was a much more reasonable supposition, and it posed the further question — where had Renshaw been?

The answer to that could only be found when it was discovered what had happened to the man after he had walked out of the gates of Broadmoor in the postman's uniform, and vanished from sight. What *could* have happened to him? It had been in broad daylight, and he couldn't have got very far before the alarm was given and everybody in the district was looking for him — for a man in a postman's uniform. Quite a conspicuous object, when you came to think of it. Mr. Budd had a theory concerning Renshaw's disappearance, but it didn't help — in fact, it only made things more complicated.

He sighed and stubbed out the butt of his cigar in the ashtray on the table beside his bed. He had felt that this case was going to be difficult at the beginning — and he'd been right.

He hoisted himself off the bed and began to undress. His review of the case had not resulted in much, he thought, but it was getting late, and he had the interview with Colonel Blair to face in the morning.

It was a long time before he fell asleep; and when he did eventually, his slumbers were disturbed by uneasy dreams in which he pursued the melancholy Leek, who was carrying a great coil of red tape with which he entangled Mr. Budd, so that he was unable to move, while somewhere in the background lurked a shadowy figure without a face that laughed discordantly.

* * *

'Sit down, Superintendent,' said Colonel Blair. Mr. Budd lowered himself gingerly on to the chair in front of the assistant commissioner's desk.

'I should like you to tell me what progress you've made in this red tape business,' said Colonel Blair. 'Your written report will, of course, reach me in due course, but I thought we could have a little chat over the matter.'

'Yes, sir,' said Mr. Budd.

'I realise all the difficulties that you have to contend with in a case of this kind,' went on the assistant commissioner, smoothing his already immaculate grey hair with the palm of one hand. 'But unless we can offer some statement soon, there will be the usual outcry in the newspapers about the inefficiency of the police. Have you anything that I can give the public information officer that he can release to the press?'

Mr. Budd shook his head slowly. 'I'm afraid not, sir. I'll tell you the position as it stands at present.' He proceeded to do so, going over all the steps he had taken and the facts he had discovered in detail.

'Well, you certainly don't appear to have neglected any possibility,' said Colonel Blair when he had finished. 'What are you proposing to do next?'

Mr. Budd leaned forward, resting a podgy hand on the edge of the desk. 'I've told you all the facts, sir,' he said slowly. 'Now I'd like to tell you somethin' else. I'd like to tell you what I *think*. I want you to understand that I've no *evidence* for what I'm goin' to say. It's only an idea that struck me in the early hours of this mornin'.'

Colonel Blair looked at him curiously. 'Are you going to tell me that you've found the answer to this business?'

'I wish I could say yes to that. No, sir, I don't know who this red tape killer is; but I've an idea that we've been lookin' at it the wrong way.'

The assistant commissioner wrinkled his smooth forehead. 'I don't understand you, Superintendent. How do you mean, the wrong way?'

'What I mean, sir,' explained Mr. Budd carefully, 'is this. That there may be somethin' behind these murders that we haven't spotted — somethin' quite simple.'

'Go on.'

'That's all, sir,' answered Mr. Budd. 'I haven't got any further than that.'

'Do you mean that it may not have anything to do with Renshaw and Penfold after all?'

'I'm not sayin' that it hasn't got anythin' to do with them. But it may not have anythin' to do with 'em *in the way we think it has*, if you understand what I mean.'

Colonel Blair picked up his pencil, looked at it, pursed his lips, and put it down again. 'You say you've no evidence to support this idea?'

'None whatever, sir. It's just an idea, that's all.'

'It's not the first time you've had these 'ideas'. There usually turns out to be a lot of truth in them. Can you suggest what this — er — quite simple motive could be?'

'Maybe I could hazard a wild guess, sir; but I'd rather not, if you don't mind.'

Colonel Blair smiled. With two fingers he stroked the closely clipped moustache above his upper lip. 'I think I've known you long enough not to press you. I've told you before that I have every confidence in your ability. It's only on very rare occasions that you fail. Let me know as soon as you've something definite.'

'Thank you, sir.'

As he walked ponderously back to his own office, Mr. Budd hoped fervently that he would be able to think of something that would justify the assistant commissioner's faith in him.

11

Sergeant Leek had not arrived when Mr. Budd reached his office, but he came in a few minutes later with a very long face and a more melancholy expression than ever.

'I'm feelin' terrible,' he announced in a lugubrious voice.

'You're lookin' it. What's the matter with yer now?'

'I 'aven't slept a wink,' complained the sergeant. 'Not a wink, I 'aven't! All night long I've been lyin' awake, starin' at the ceilin'.'

'Well, I s'pose nature's bound to catch up on yer sometimes. You can't spend *all* your life asleep.'

'It's this 'ere case that's doin' it. I can't get it out of me mind.'

'Don't tell me you're gettin' conscientious. I can't believe it.'

'It's worryin' me. I can't 'elp thinkin' about that feller Renshaw.'

'Well, I'm glad to hear that, because I've got a job for you.'

'I'm not fit to do anythin' today,' declared Leek.

'You're not fit to do anythin' any day,' snarled Mr. Budd, 'but you're goin' to do this, so you'd better pull yourself together!'

'It's nothin' more than slavery, that's what it is,' said the sergeant miserably. 'Goin' back to Uncle Tom's cabin, that's what's 'appenin'.'

'You're not goin' to Uncle Tom's cabin, or even Aunt Fanny's bungalow!' snapped Mr. Budd crossly. 'I'll tell you what you're goin' to do.' He proceeded to do so, and the unhappy Leek listened, his long face growing longer with every sentence.

'It may take days,' he grumbled when Mr. Budd came to the end of his instructions.

'Days, weeks, months,' said Mr. Budd inexorably. 'It doesn't matter. I want it done. You can have all the assistance that's necessary.'

'I don't see that it's goin' ter do much good. They must've done all that at the time.'

'Maybe. But p'raps they didn't do enough. Now get goin', an' phone me if you have any luck.'

* * *

'Look at this,' snorted Mr. Sorbet, glaring at the copy that Peter Ashton had put on his desk. 'Look at it!'

'I've been looking at it,' said Peter coolly. 'How could I write it without looking at it?'

'How could you write it at all?' demanded the irate news editor. 'It's muck — sheer, unadulterated muck! You call yourself a crime reporter and this is the best you can do? There's nothing *new* here. It's just a lot of rehashing. I want something startling. Sensational.'

'What about doubling my salary?'

Mr. Sorbet very nearly foamed at the mouth. 'I'll tell you something,' he grated through his teeth. 'If you don't give me something better than this rubbish, you won't be getting a salary at all!'

'Now don't work yourself up,' interposed Peter soothingly. 'You know it only gives you indigestion! I can't do miracles. I can't *make* news. I can only report what happens.'

'Go out and find something!' snapped the news editor. 'What are the police doing? What's that friend of yours, Budd, doing? What line of inquiry is being followed? Is this red tape maniac really a lunatic with a grudge against the legal profession, or is there something else behind these crimes? Give me a fresh angle.'

'You'll have to be patient,' said Peter. 'You'll have the exclusive story when it breaks.'

'How long will that be?'

Peter shrugged his shoulders. 'How do you expect me to answer that? All I can tell you is that we shall have the story twenty-four hours before any other newspaper. I've got Budd's promise on that.'

Mr, Sorbet looked at him suspiciously, but his expression was slightly more mollified.

'Hm,' he grunted. 'If it isn't soon, the public will have lost interest. Can't you unearth something to keep the thing going?'

'I've hinted that there may shortly be sensational developments.'

'I know, I know — all the old stuff. The public's got used to that. We want something concrete, not just hints.'

'I'll go and murder the advertisement manager,' said Peter helpfully.

'I wish you would.'

'You've no conscience.'

'I couldn't do this job if I had. It's a pity this maniac didn't choose reporters instead of lawyers — that would have been news!'

'Without any reporters there wouldn't *be* any news,' remarked Peter truthfully, and he left Mr. Sorbet to get on with his work.

It was quite true, he thought as he left the offices of the *Morning Mail*. The column he had turned in *was* rubbish. It contained nothing fresh, and somehow or other he would have to follow it up with something better. He considered going along to the Yard to see Mr. Budd, but decided that it might be wiser to leave him alone for a bit. Perhaps there might be something to be picked up from the backgrounds of the three victims. He might be able to acquire enough to work up into an interesting article. Since the offices of Messrs. Gamble, Gamble, Chalkit and Gamble were the nearest, he decided to start with Timothy Smithson.

Miss Catkin was busily typing when he entered the outer office, and she looked up quickly.

'My name is Ashton, Peter Ashton,' said the reporter. 'I'm from the *Morning Mail*.'

'Oh dear,' replied Miss Catkin, 'are you *another* reporter? We've had so *many* of them since poor Mr. Smithson was murdered.'

That doesn't sound very hopeful, thought Peter. *The ground has been thoroughly ploughed already. I should have come along here yesterday, instead of wasting my time with Budd.* Aloud, he said: 'I'm very sorry to disturb you, but if you wouldn't mind answering a few questions, I'd be very grateful.'

'Oh, I don't mind at all,' answered Miss

Catkin, who really rather enjoyed this unusual notoriety. 'I've already had my photograph taken twice. I think it's going to be used in an interview.'

'That will be nice for you,' said Peter, and wondered which enterprising newspaper had thought of *that* one. The *Mail* wouldn't have touched it, anyway. 'You've been working as secretary with this firm for quite a long time, haven't you?'

'Oh, yes, for many, many years. I started soon after Mr. Humphrey took over.'

'It must have been a great shock to you when Mr. Gamble was murdered.'

'Indeed it was,' declared Miss Catkin fervently. 'And then for poor Mr. Smithson to suffer the same fate so soon afterwards. It made me quite ill. I haven't really recovered from the shock yet.'

'It must have been terribly upsetting for you,' said Peter sympathetically. 'Were you surprised when you learned that Mr. Gamble had left a will in favour of Mr. Smithson?'

'I certainly thought he should have left a great deal more to his sister. After all, she spent the greater part of her life looking after him. I think it was most unfair.'

'He left her an annuity.'

Miss Catkin sniffed. It was a very delicate and genteel sniff, but definitely a sniff. 'It was a very small one,' she replied.

'Who'll benefit now that Mr. Smithson is dead?'

Miss Catkin shook her head. 'I don't really know.'

'Didn't he leave a will?' persisted Peter. There might be something here that would give him a new item to work on.

'Nothing of the kind has been found. I suppose it will all go to his next of kin. I don't know what will happen to the business. I suppose it'll be sold.' She sighed. 'I expect that'll mean that I shall have to look for another job.'

'Probably the people who take it over will ask you to remain. Who is the next of kin, do you know?'

'Mr. Smithson's half-sister, Mrs. Bristow.'

'That's the mother of the woman who was engaged to Richard Penfold, the man who shot himself a year ago, isn't it?' said Peter, who knew perfectly well that it was. 'Who's looking after the business at the moment?'

'Mr. Grindthorpe. He was a friend of Mr. Gamble's. Would you like to see him? He's in the office.' She nodded towards the closed door.

As though by some telepathic communication between them, the door opened, and Mr. Grindthorpe appeared on the threshold. He was carrying a piece of paper in his hand and he looked excited. 'Miss Catkin,' he cried, 'I've found it!'

'Oh my goodness, *what* have you found, Mr. Grindthorpe?' gasped Miss Catkin.

'Smithson's will!' declared the cherubic lawyer, waving the piece of paper. 'Here it is, dated the day before he was killed. I found it between the pages of the big ledger in the safe. Smithson has left everything to Miss Gamble.'

'Oh, I'm *so* glad,' exclaimed Miss Catkin. 'I *really* am. She did so deserve to get it.'

'Well, she's got it, or she *will* have it as

soon as this will's been proved,' said Mr. Grindthorpe. 'There'll be no difficulty about that, eh? It's perfectly in order, signed and properly witnessed.'

Peter thanked his stars for this bit of luck. This was exclusive information that would give him just what he wanted. Mr. Grindthorpe caught sight of him at that moment. He had been too excited over his discovery to notice him before.

'Who's this?' he asked.

Miss Catkin opened her mouth to explain, but Peter forestalled her. 'I'm from the *Morning Mail*, Mr. Grindthorpe. I was just going to ask if I could see you.'

'A reporter, eh? I suppose you heard what I said just now, eh? Couldn't very well help it, could you?'

'I certainly did hear,' admitted the reporter. 'There's no particular reason why the matter should be kept a secret, is there?'

Mr. Grindthorpe pursed his lips. 'No, I can't see any reason. Suppose you want to publish it in your paper, eh? No reason why you shouldn't, you know. Soon become public property, anyway, eh? Go ahead, if you want to. Get Miss Gamble on the telephone if you can, Miss Catkin. I'll take the call in my office.' He nodded to Peter and disappeared into the inner office.

'I'll be going,' said Peter hastily as Miss Catkin went over to the telephone. 'Thanks for all your trouble.'

He hurried down the stairs to the street and looked round for a taxi. There wasn't one in sight, and he walked quickly to the junction with the main road. Here, he was luckier. He spotted a cab for hire on the other side of the street and hailed it. A few seconds later, he was *en route* to Wellington Park and the home of the late Humphrey Gamble. If he could get an interview with Emily Gamble, just after the news had reached her about Timothy Smithson's will, it ought to satisfy even the rapacious demands of Mr. Sorbet.

Emily Gamble opened the door herself to his ring. There was a faint flush in her usually sallow cheeks, and her eyes were a little brighter.

'You're the young man from the

Morning Mail, aren't you?' she greeted. 'Mr. Grindthorpe told me you'd probably be calling.'

Peter grinned. There were no flies on Grindthorpe, he thought. He'd guessed what he would do.

'That's right, Miss Gamble,' he said. 'I was in the office when the will was found. Let me congratulate you on your good fortune.'

'Is it good fortune?' asked Miss Gamble a little doubtfully. 'Of course, I'm very grateful to Mr. Smithson. It was most kind of him to think of me. But I'm a very lonely woman. I miss my brother, and nothing can bring him back. Won't you come in?'

'Thank you,' said Peter, and she led him into the lounge.

'Why did you come all the way from London to see me?' she asked.

'I wanted to get your reaction to the news,' he said candidly.

She looked a trifle puzzled. 'My reaction?'

'Yes, the readers of the *Morning Mail* will be interested. What are your plans for the future? Are you going to dispose of the business? Do you intend to stay here, or to move to another house?'

She seemed rather disconcerted. 'I — er — don't know. I haven't thought about it. It's been rather sudden. Of course, I *was* going to sell this house. My annuity wasn't large enough to keep it. And I don't know that I wish to — to live here, now that my brother isn't here.'

'It holds too many memories?' suggested the reporter.

She nodded slowly. 'Yes, indeed.'

'You'll be in a position to do anything you like now. Have you had any special desire — anything you very much wanted to do?'

She looked at him thoughtfully. She had a thin face, scraped-back hair and angular figure. And yet there was something pathetic about her. Peter noticed that her large and knuckly hands were rough and reddened from work. She had spent most of her life looking after her brother, keeping the house clean and cooking his meals.

'I think I should like to travel,' she said

at last, but there was no real conviction in her voice. 'I've always wanted to see more of the world. Yes, I should like to travel abroad, from one place to another.' She smiled a little wanly. 'I don't suppose I ever shall. I should feel rather lost.'

'It would probably do you a great deal of good. You could always engage a companion, you know, and you'd meet a lot of fresh people and make friends.'

'I've never had many friends. Joseph — Mr. Grindthorpe — is the only really intimate friend we had.'

'It's time you started, then. Did it surprise you to hear that Mr. Smithson had left you everything?'

'Yes, indeed it did,' she said. 'Of course, I've known him for a considerable time, but I wouldn't describe him as a friend. I don't remember meeting him very often. He came here once or twice, you know, to see Humphrey on business; and I've seen him when I've been in London, shopping, and called at the office.'

'You've no idea why he should have made a will in your favour?'

'Only out of kindness. Or perhaps he

thought the money and the business should go to a member of the family.'

'Your brother didn't think that?'

'My brother had a very high opinion of Mr. Smithson. I think he thought the money and the business would be better in his hands than in mine. He thought a woman's place was in the house, and that she was quite incapable of looking after money.'

From what he had heard, Peter concluded that the late Humphrey Gamble must have been very difficult to live with. He had got the basis for a pretty good article, however, and he was anxious to get back to the offices of the *Morning Mail*. On the way, he would call in at the Yard on the chance that Mr. Budd might have some further information.

A few minutes later he said goodbye to Miss Gamble and, since there was no likelihood of picking up a cab in the vicinity of the house, walked to the station where he found a taxi in the approach.

Mr. Budd was in his office when he reached the Yard, and greeted him without much enthusiasm. 'I nearly sent down to say I couldn't see you,' he grunted, 'but a mistaken kindness got the better of me good judgement. What d'you want this mornin'?'

'I wondered if there were any further developments,' said Peter. 'I'm just on my way back to the *Mail*.'

'Where've you been gadding about to?'

'I've been to see Miss Emily Gamble. Smithson left her everything. Grindthorpe found his will in the safe.'

'You don't neglect anythin', do you? I s'pose you're goin' to print an account of your interview for the poor half-witted people who read the *Mornin' Mail?* 'Sister of murder victim inherits fortune', eh?'

'Something of the kind.' Peter grinned. 'Any objections?'

Mr. Budd shook his head. 'No, that can't do any harm. I'm glad she's goin' to get it.'

'Any news of Renshaw?'

Again the superintendent shook his head.

'Well, I suppose you're doing something,' said Peter. 'You're not just sitting here waiting for the murderer to walk in the door, are you?'

Mr. Budd did not appear to have heard him. With half-closed eyes, he had slumped back in his chair, his many chins sunk on his chest.

'Hi!' cried Peter. 'Have you gone to sleep?'

Mr. Budd opened one eye and regarded him malevolently. 'I'm just thinkin'. Action's all right when you know what action you're goin' to take. I don't — yet.'

Peter laughed. 'Right you are. I won't disturb you any longer. Just let me know when you go into action, will you? I'd like to be there.'

'You'll know,' grunted Mr. Budd, and he closed his eye again.

* * *

It was a small thing that put Mr. Budd on the right track and eventually led him to the truth. Actually, the hazy idea must have been lurking in his subconscious mind, but it was not until he read a certain word in his evening paper that it swam up out of the depths into full and startling clarity. Even then it only existed as a vague and rather improbable possibility, but Mr. Budd had learned from experience never to pass over anything, however unlikely it appeared at first sight.

The paragraph was quite short and concerned an accident between a motor car and a bicycle which had been witnessed by a youth on his way home from work, but it started a train of circumstances that led to the apprehension of the red tape murderer.

As soon as he reached his home, Mr. Budd put through a telephone call. To the person who answered, he asked a question which was received in some surprise at the other end of the wire.

'I'm not sure that I can remember,' came the answer, after a pause. 'I could let you know tomorrow, if it's important.'

'That'll do,' said Mr. Budd. 'Let me know as early as you can.'

'What's the idea?' inquired the voice over the telephone, curiously.

223

'Just that,' answered Mr. Budd, 'an idea — '

He hung up the receiver before he could be asked any more questions.

After his evening meal, he settled himself down to turn over in his mind the startling potentiality of the suggestion which had so suddenly occurred to him.

12

The information that Mr. Budd had asked for over the telephone reached him at a quarter to eleven on the following morning. At ten minutes to eleven, he left Scotland Yard to find out whether his theory was correct or not. He was gone for a considerable time; but when he eventually returned, there was elation in his heart. He knew the identity of the red tape murderer!

But there was still a great deal of work to be done before he could prove it. He hadn't sufficient evidence to take before a jury, and it wasn't going to be easy to get. It would have to be handled very carefully, if the killer wasn't to slip through his fingers.

Mr. Budd lit one of his black cigars and frowned. What was the best way to go about it? Whatever it was, it must provide irrefutable proof. There would be no second chance.

He evolved several schemes, but discarded them one after another. They all fell down on the one essential point — the proof wouldn't be certain. There would still remain an element of doubt.

It was late in the afternoon before he hit on a possible plan. If it came off, the proof would be absolutely final — sufficient to satisfy the most sceptical of juries. But would it come off? Would the killer react in the way expected? That was a risk that had to be taken.

Mr. Budd was still sitting and cogitating when Leek came in. The sergeant looked tired and dispirited.

'Well?' asked the superintendent. 'What are you doin' here? Any news?'

Leek shook his head. 'Nothin'. If you want my opinion — '

'I don't,' cut in Mr. Budd curtly. 'All I want from you is to get on with the job.'

'I've got to 'ave a bit of a rest,' protested Leek. 'It's a tirin' job.'

'You stick at it. I want to know, one way or the other, as soon as possible.'

'I'm doin' me best. But I think you're on the wrong track.'

'Oh, you do, do you? Well, maybe you're right. But you can still go on tryin'.' He reached out a podgy hand, took a sheet of paper from the rack on his desk, and picking up a pen, began to write slowly.

'What are you doin'?' asked the sergeant.

'I'm writin' a letter,' replied Mr. Budd without looking up. 'I'm writin' a letter to the killer.'

Leek's jaw dropped, so that his long face looked longer than ever. 'What did you say?'

'I said I was writin' to the killer.'

'D'you mean — you know who it is?' asked the sergeant incredulously.

Mr. Budd nodded. 'Oh, yes, I know.'

'What are you writin' to him for?'

'I'm suggestin' that there might be another murder,' replied Mr. Budd calmly.

★   ★   ★

Mr. Joseph Grindthorpe, his usual cherubic expression replaced by a worried

227

frown, stared at the letter on the writing table. What was the best thing to do about it? It wasn't the sort of thing that he could make up his mind about immediately. It would require a great deal of thought. But he would definitely have to do something about it. The matter was urgent. For his own safety, he would have to come to a decision as quickly as possible.

He got up and began to pace up and down the office. It was no longer the dusty and untidy place in which Humphrey Gamble had spent the greater part of his life. With the assistance of Miss Catkin, Mr. Grindthorpe had brought a certain order and neatness out of the previous chaos. But he wasn't concerned with the alteration in his surroundings. He went back to the writing table and read the letter again. It was incredible! All his instincts warned him to ignore it, but he knew that he dare not. He'd have to take action, whatever the risk.

Miss Catkin came in with a cup of tea, and he hastily covered the letter from her curious eyes. 'That appointment with Mr. Boardman over the Lancing property,' he said. 'Would you telephone and say that I'm afraid it'll have to be postponed until tomorrow? Make any excuse you like.'

Miss Catkin looked surprised. 'Mr. Boardman is due in an hour,' she said. 'I don't know whether I can catch him at his office.'

'You must try,' said Mr. Grindthorpe firmly. 'If you can't stop him coming here, you must put him off when he arrives, eh? I've got to go out — a very urgent matter.'

Miss Catkin promised to do her best. When she had retired again to the outer office, Mr. Grindthorpe picked up the letter, folded it, and put it in his pocket. Putting on his overcoat and hat, he went out into the outer office.

'I don't know what time I'll be back, Miss Catkin,' he said. 'I may not be able to return at all today. If I don't, lock up as usual, will you?'

When he had gone, Miss Catkin went into the inner office to telephone to Mr. Boardman. It was more comfortable than using her own instrument. The first thing she saw was the cup of tea she had taken in a few moments before. It was untasted.

'Well,' she muttered to herself, 'fancy that! What *can* be the matter with Mr. Grindthorpe? Something must have upset him.'

★ ★ ★

Mr. Budd surveyed the two detective-constables before him sleepily. 'You know what you've got ter do?' he said. 'This feller's got to be kept under close observation from now on. One or other of you has got to follow 'im wherever he goes. Understand?'

'Yes, sir.' The answer came from both the men almost at the same time.

'Whatever you do, don't lose sight of him. I shan't listen to any excuses. An' it mustn't be noticeable that he's bein' trailed. If you don't carry out yer instructions prop'ly, there may be another red tape killin' an' you'll be responsible.'

They assured him that his instructions would be carried out implicitly.

'They'd better be. Now, go an' get busy.'

Peter Ashton was in the reporters' room at the offices of the *Morning Mail* when the telephone message came through.

'Hello,' he said into the mouthpiece. 'What gave you sufficient energy to phone, eh?'

'If you're goin' to be rude,' answered the voice of Mr. Budd over the wire, 'I'll ring off.'

'Don't do that,' broke in Peter hastily. 'If it wasn't something important, you wouldn't've phoned. What is it?'

'I just thought you might like to be in at the death,' said Mr. Budd.

'What d'you mean?'

'I promised you I'd give you the exclusive story of the red tape murders, didn't I? Well, I always like keepin' me promises.'

'Are you telling me that you've cracked the case?'

'I know practically everythin',' said Mr. Budd calmly. 'I'll know *all* about it tonight. I thought maybe you'd like ter come an' see the arrest.'

'Who is it?'

'If you come along, you'll see for yerself. I'm not tellin' you anythin' now.'

'Nothing short of an atomic explosion 'ud keep me away,' declared the reporter. 'Where?'

'You'd better pick me up at the Yard at seven o'clock. An' don't be late!'

'I'll be there. You're a great man, Budd — in more senses than one.'

'If you start any of your corny jokes,' threatened Mr. Budd, 'I'll call it off.'

'I really mean it,' said Peter. 'If you've found the red tape murderer, you really are a great man.'

'I'll know just 'ow great I am after tonight's over.'

'How did you get on to him?'

'By just sittin' an' thinkin'.'

'It's a method that seems to work with you. It wouldn't with everybody.'

'Most people just sit,' retorted Mr. Budd, and he rang off.

* * *

A thin mist descended on London with the coming of evening and threatened to grow thicker as the night advanced. Mr. Grindthorpe had been nervous and ill at ease all the afternoon, to the obvious surprise and curiosity of Miss Catkin. She couldn't make it out. It had started on the previous day and had been steadily growing worse. It was so unlike Mr. Grindthorpe. He was usually so placid and good-humoured. She wondered what could have happened. Earlier, she had asked him if he was feeling ill and he had nearly snapped her head off. Really quite rude, he'd been.

Perhaps, she thought, it was the strain of having to look after two businesses. But he hadn't spent much time at his own office since the death of Timothy Smithson. He'd left that to his managing clerk — a very nice man, much younger than Mr. Smithson had been — who brought round anything that he couldn't deal with himself. No, it must be some private worry, Miss Catkin decided. If he'd been married, she would have thought it was domestic trouble, but of course he wasn't.

It was all very perplexing. Miss Catkin's bump of inquisitiveness was so extremely well-developed that it wouldn't let her rest. On every possible excuse, she popped into the inner office, hoping that she might discover some clue to Mr. Grindthorpe's strange behaviour. But she was disappointed. At half-past five, Mr. Grindthorpe announced his intention of leaving.

'I haven't finished the letters yet,' said Miss Catkin.

'Then they'll have to wait until the morning, eh?' said Mr. Grindthorpe. 'Good night, Miss Catkin.'

Miss Catkin looked after his disappearing back in dismay. What on earth could be the matter? There were several important letters that should have caught the evening post. Could it be that Mr. Grindthorpe was a secret drinker? She had never suspected such a thing before, and there was certainly no smell of alcohol about him, but there must be some explanation for his peculiar conduct. She shook her head. It really *was* very strange.

Mr. Grindthorpe came out of the main doorway of the offices and paused for a moment on the pavement, peering through the thin mist. It was very cold and damp. He was glad of the heavy overcoat he was wearing, otherwise he rather welcomed the fog. It might help him in doing what he had to do.

The man who was reading a newspaper under the light of a lamp on the other side of the street was not so pleased. The mist wasn't so bad, now, but if it got thicker . . . ?

As Mr. Grindthorpe moved off up the street, the man with the newspaper folded it up, thrust it into his pocket, and followed. The figure of the stout little lawyer was easily distinguishable among the crowd of homeward-bound workers hurrying to catch Tubes and busses. He appeared to be in no particular hurry, and the trailer had little difficulty in keeping him in sight.

At the corner of the street, where it came out into the main thoroughfare, there was a public house, and Mr. Grindthorpe, after a moment's hesitation, entered the saloon bar. The man who was following him did the same. The lawyer ordered a double scotch, poured into it a small quantity of water, and gulped it down quickly. He looked at his watch and then at the clock behind the bar, before he ordered another drink. This he drank more slowly, sipping it and twisting the glass nervously in his fingers.

The trailer, at the other end of the bar, slowly drank the half-pint of bitter he had ordered and lit a cigarette. It was better in here than out in the damp fog, he thought. Where was the chap going from here? he wondered.

He soon found out. Quite suddenly, Mr. Grindthorpe finished the remainder of his drink and made for the door. A bus was passing as he emerged into the street, momentarily held up by the traffic, and the lawyer jumped on board. The man who was following him had to run hard to catch up with the bus, which accelerated at the same moment. He just made it, and was clutching on to a strap in the crowded interior, when the conductor came down the steps from the upper deck.

'Here,' he said, 'there's too many of yer in here. Where did you get on?'

'Just now,' answered the trailer.

'Yer'll 'ave ter get off at the next stop.'

'What about the other feller?' demanded the trailer. 'He got on at the same time as I did.'

'He was lucky. There was one seat on top.'

'Can't I just stand here? I'm not taking up much room.'

'Sorry, mate. I got too many standin' already.'

The trailer slipped his hand in his breast pocket. 'Take a look at this,' he whispered, and held the warrant card in front of the conductor's nose. 'It's important that I stay on this bus.'

'Okay,' said the man after a quick look at the card, 'but you'll have to explain to the inspector if he gets on. There's been a bit o' trouble about overcrowdin' lately.'

'I'll make it all right,' said the trailer. 'Maybe I won't be bothering you long.'

'What're yer on?' asked the conductor under his breath.

'Can't tell you that.'

'Chappie upstairs, eh?' muttered the conductor. 'Yer needn't answer that, mate. I ain't curious.'

Mr. Grindthorpe made no effort to get off the bus until it was nearing Victoria Station, and then he began to descend the stairs. As it came to a stop, he dropped off the step and hurried towards the station entrance.

The trailer followed him quickly, with a parting wink from the bus conductor. He was close behind him when he bought his ticket at the booking office, and bought a similar one. The train was in and it was crowded. Mr. Grindthorpe managed to squeeze himself into one compartment, however, and his shadow was lucky enough to find room a little farther along.

A few minutes later, the train pulled out from the platform and faded from view in the mist.

* * *

Peter Ashton arrived at Scotland Yard a quarter of an hour before the time of his appointment with Mr. Budd, but the superintendent was in his office, and he was shown up.

'You're a bit early,' remarked Mr. Budd.

'I want to hear all about it,' said Peter. 'Who is it you're going to arrest? Have you found Renshaw? What did — '

'Now just a minute,' expostulated Mr. Budd, holding up a hand in protest. 'I'm not answerin' any questions, so it's no good you firin' 'em at me like that.'

'Do you mean that now I'm here, you're not going to tell me anything?'

'That's right,' agreed Mr. Budd complacently. 'I'm not tellin' you anythin'. I'm goin' ter *show* you.'

'You're going to show me the red tape murderer? What do you mean? Is he coming here?'

Mr. Budd shook his head. 'No. In a few minutes, you an' me's goin' on a little trip. At the end of it, I'm hopin' to meet the killer.'

'Where are we going?'

'You'll see when we get there. I'm bein' very kind to you, Ashton. I'm givin' you the story of yer life.' Mr. Budd hoisted himself out of his chair and pulled on his overcoat. 'It's time we was startin'. I've got a police car waitin' down below.'

'Isn't Leek coming with us?'

'He's busy elsewhere,' replied Mr. Budd, reaching for his hat. 'Come on, let's get goin'.'

The driver of the police car had evidently already received his instructions, for he drove off as soon as they were inside. The mist was thickening, and this seemed to cause Mr. Budd some uneasiness, for he grunted irritably to himself.

'Is it going to spoil your plans?' said the reporter.

'It might make things very awkward if it gets too thick,' muttered Mr. Budd, peering out of the window.

By the time they had left central London behind, Peter had lost his sense of direction. He couldn't have said where they were heading, but the driver never appeared to be in doubt. Smoothly, and at a fair speed considering the fog, the car continued on its way, twisting and turning through a maze of side streets until eventually it slowed and came to a stop in a dark road that was completely unfamiliar to Peter.

'Here we are, sir,' announced the police driver.

Mr. Budd opened the door and got heavily out. 'Come on,' he said curtly to Peter. 'You stay here, Fielding. We'll be back soon.'

'Okay, sir,' said the driver.

'We've got to walk from here,' grunted Mr. Budd, moving off into the mist and darkness. 'An' we've got to be careful.'

'Where are we?' asked Peter, peering about to try and find something familiar that would tell him.

'You'll see,' said Mr. Budd evasively. 'Now, don't talk any more. Voices carry. I don't want to scare our bird off.'

Peter relapsed into silence. He was consumed with curiosity, but obviously the superintendent knew what he was doing.

They turned into another road equally

unfamiliar to the reporter, negotiated a narrow passage that ran between the back gardens of two rows of houses, and found themselves halfway along a wider road, the dim lights of which shone blearily through the mist.

Mr. Budd stopped. 'There's a house here,' he whispered in so low a tone that Peter found it difficult to catch what he said. 'It's got a hedge.'

He found the place a few yards farther along and cautiously opened the gate. He motioned Peter into the front garden and followed him, closing the gate without latching it. The reporter saw that there was a light in the front windows of the house. He expected that Mr. Budd would go up the path to the front door, but he apparently had no such intention. He seemed to have no interest in this house at all.

Taking the reporter's arm, he led him behind the privet hedge, and pressed him gently into the shadow of a bush.

'This'll do,' he whispered with his lips close to Peter's ear. 'Don't make a sound.'

They waited, crouching in the damp

garden behind the hedge. The white wreaths of mist curled sluggishly round them, growing thicker as the time went by. There was no sound except Mr. Budd's heavy breathing and an occasional car passing along the road beyond.

The seconds ticked away. Peter looked at the watch on his wrist and saw to his surprise that it was only ten minutes to eight. He thought that it must have stopped, but when he held it to his ear he found that it was still going. It scarcely seemed possible that it was less than an hour since they had left Scotland Yard.

Suddenly, he felt Mr. Budd beside him stiffen. Mr. Budd's arm was touching his and the muscles had gone rigid. A faint sound reached him: a sound that was almost inaudible.

From somewhere in the mist and darkness came footsteps. They were coming down the road in the direction of the hedge behind which Peter and the superintendent were hiding.

Nearer and nearer they came, the firm steps of a man . . .

Peter heard Mr. Budd's breath hiss

through his teeth. So this was what they had been waiting for, thought the reporter. This must be the red tape murderer!

A shadowy figure, only slightly darker than the darkness that surrounded it, loomed up by the gate. It passed by, misty and vague, but unmistakably that of a man, and was swallowed up in the thickening fog.

Mr. Budd straightened up quickly. With remarkable agility for a man of his build, he was out of the gate and crossing the road. Peter followed him. Mr. Budd was moving swiftly and silently along the pavement on the other side of the road, in the direction taken by the man who had passed the hedge.

Peter, wondering what was going to happen next, kept up with Mr. Budd. He could hear the sound of the other man's footsteps again, almost parallel with them, on the opposite pavement; but the man himself was invisible in the mist.

And then he heard something else. Other footsteps, soft and muffled, that came from *behind them*!

Peter drew closer to Mr. Budd and whispered in his ear, but the superintendent took no notice. He had slightly quickened his pace. The reporter looked back. There was a lamp standard several yards behind, and he caught a glimpse of a distorted shadow thrown by the feeble light on the curtain of mist. Even as he looked, it merged with the darkness beyond the rays of light and was gone.

But his attention was distracted from the shadowy figure *behind* them by the behaviour of Mr. Budd. He had stopped and was leaning slightly forward, listening intently. Peter listened too, but he could hear nothing.

The footsteps of the man on the other side of the road had stopped! So had the soft and muffled footsteps behind . . .

They had moved into a patch of fog that was thicker here than it had been anywhere. He couldn't see anything at all through the white blanket that swirled round them. But he could hear . . . The sound of voices reached him, indistinct and unreal; a faint murmur that sounded curiously deadened. It came from the opposite side of the road.

'I'm here, sir,' whispered a voice almost at his elbow, and the startled Peter jumped. Noiselessly, a man had joined them and was standing just behind him. 'What do you want me to do?'

'Nothin' — for the moment,' answered Mr. Budd in the same almost inaudible whisper. 'We've got to be careful.'

He was still leaning forward, peering into the fog, and listening. Peter felt his pulse quicken. The man who had joined them must be one of Mr. Budd's own men. That was why he had taken no notice when the reporter had drawn his attention to him.

The voices on the other side of the road had ceased. There was now only silence. Mr. Budd moved forward, swiftly and without a sound. From the pocket of his heavy overcoat he drew out a large torch. With Peter and the other man close behind him, he went quickly and stealthily across the road.

And suddenly the silence was broken by the shrill blast of a whistle! A light, dim and hazy in the mist, flashed out in front of them. Mr. Budd's torch blazed to life, cutting a sword-like swath through the white vapour, and was joined by another from a similar torch in the hand of the man beside him. Peter heard a sharp, startled cry. Hurried running footsteps reached his ears from the screening fog. More lights sprang up in the darkness, moved, and converged to form one brilliant pool that focused on a running figure that loomed out of the mist.

The beam from Mr. Budd's torch swung upwards, catching and holding in its light a white, strained, distorted face.

Peter's heart gave a sudden bound as he saw that the face belonged to Emily Gamble.

★ ★ ★

Mr. Budd sat behind his desk in his office at Scotland Yard, sipping the cup of hot coffee that he had ordered from the canteen. Peter occupied the chair that was usually used by Leek, his cup balanced on his knee. It was a little after ten, and a lot had happened since he had seen that white face burst out of the fog into the light of Mr. Budd's torch.

Emily Gamble, tight-lipped and silent, had been arrested and charged with the murder of Humphrey Gamble, Charles Gilmore and Timothy Smithson, and the attempted murder of Joseph Grindthorpe. Mr. Grindthorpe, unconscious, and with the red tape already round his throat, had been removed from the waste ground where Humphrey Gamble had met his death, and taken to hospital to recover from the drug that had been administered to him. Except for the effects of that, and the shock of being nearly strangled, he was uninjured.

Peter's astonishment at the climax to the night's activities had been complete. What he had expected he couldn't have said, but what actually happened had come as a devastating surprise. There had been no time to question Mr. Budd during the rather hectic proceedings that had followed Emily Gamble's arrest, but now that it was all over, his curiosity couldn't be held in check any longer.

'Now then,' he said, 'perhaps you'll explain.'

Mr. Budd finished his coffee and pushed aside the empty cup. 'What d'you want to know?' he asked with a prodigious yawn.

'I want to know everything. What put you on to Emily Gamble? Why did she kill these three men? How did you know she was planning to kill Grindthorpe? Why — '

'Now hold on, Mr. Ashton,' protested Mr. Budd. 'I can't answer all these questions at once. As a matter of fact, it was *you* who put me on to Emily Gamble as bein' the murderess.'

'Me?' exclaimed Peter. 'How on earth could it have been me?'

'When you told me about the will. Yer see, it struck me as peculiar that Smithson shouldn't've got Miss Catkin to witness it. She was on the spot, an' she didn't benefit from it, so she would have been the *natural* person to ask. But she didn't know anythin' about it, or she'd've mentioned it. But she didn't — she didn't know that Smithson had *made* a will.'

'He might not have wanted her to know that he was leaving everything to Emily Gamble,' interposed Peter.

'At first it only struck me as peculiar,' went on Mr. Budd, ignoring the interruption. 'But I've got a tidy mind. I don't like peculiar things. I got on to Mr. Grindthorpe an' asked him the names an' addresses of the witnesses to that will. An' they was phoney — they didn't exist.'

'Do you mean that Smithson's will was a forgery?'

'Yes,' replied Mr. Budd, nodding. 'That was the motive at the back of this business, you see — money. Emily Gamble wanted money an' freedom. She'd been under the domination of 'er brother for years — no life of 'er own; suppressed. You could tell that by just lookin' at her.'

'And so she killed her brother, expecting to get the money?'

Mr. Budd shook his head. 'Oh, no she didn't. She wasn't such a fool as that. She knew that Humphrey Gamble 'ad left everythin' to Smithson. If he'd made a will in her favour, an' then been murdered, she knew that she'd've been the first suspect. She was cleverer than that. She remembered the Penfold affair. Her brother had sold 'im the land. That's how I work it out. She killed her brother. No motive pointin' to her. She killed Gilmore. Again no motive pointin' to her. She's planted the idea of a maniac killer who goes about stranglin' lawyers with red tape, an' she'd chosen two that linked up with the Penfold business to put the police off the track if they were clever enough to see the connection. Now she's ready to put into operation the *real* reason for the murders. She prepares the fake will — she must've had letters with Smithson's signature on 'em that he'd written to Gamble — an' she kills Smithson. She knows that she'll be notified of his death, an' she's got a duplicate key to the safe. Probably her brother kept one in case of accidents. She goes to the office, an' as soon as she's alone in the inner office, she opens the safe, shoves the fake will in the ledger, an' Bob's yer uncle! The scene's all set. She only has to wait for a bit, an' then she gets the lot — money, the business, everythin'.'

'What a cold-blooded plot,' exclaimed Peter. 'But what about the attempted murder of Grindthorpe? How did that fit into the plan?'

'It didn't,' said Mr. Budd calmly. 'I suggested that.'

'You suggested that he should be murdered?' cried the astonished Peter.

'Yes, in a way. You see, although I was certain that Emily Gamble was the murderess, I hadn't got any proof. There wasn't enough evidence to convince a jury. She couldn't even 'ave been convicted of forgery, since there was no proof she'd faked the will. The *probability* was that she had, because she was the beneficiary, but probability isn't proof. So I had to do somethin' that made it certain. I got hold of Grindthorpe an' I took him into my confidence. I don't think he really believed it up to the last moment, but he finally agreed to write a letter to Emily Gamble, a copy of which I wrote out for 'im statin' that he'd found that the witnesses' signatures on Smithson's will were fakes. Before doin' anythin' about the matter, he'd like to consult her. Of course, that put the cat among the pigeons, so far as she was concerned. All her careful plans would come topplin' down. She did what I hoped she'd do. She decided that Grindthorpe would have to be another victim of the red tape murderer. She telephoned him and invited him to come and see her this evening at eight o'clock. I'd arranged for him to let me know as soon as he heard anythin', an' I'd also arranged to have him watched from the moment he'd sent her that letter. I wasn't takin' any chances that she might strike before I expected her to.'

'You took a pretty big risk.'

'I know. I was sweatin' all the time. You see, I *had* to catch her in the act. It was no good her just meetin' Grindthorpe; that wouldn't've proved anythin'. We had to wait until she was actually on the point of knottin' the red tape.' Mr. Budd shook his head. 'I can tell you, I don't wish to go through those last few minutes again

— not for anythin'.'

'Well, you seem to have pulled it off,' said Peter. 'I congratulate you. You always manage to bring home the bacon, don't you? What about Renshaw? I suppose he doesn't come into it?'

'No, though I expect Leek'll find him. You see, thinkin' it over, I came to the conclusion that Renshaw never got through that cordon at all on the mornin' he escaped.'

'What happened to him, then?'

'I think he's still there. I don't mean that he's *alive*; I don't believe 'e is. But I think 'is body's still there.'

'You're full of surprises,' said Peter. He looked at the clock and jumped to his feet. 'I'll just have time to make the deadline! I can't wait to see old Sorbet's face when he hears what I've got to tell him.'

* * *

The *Mail* came out the following morning with the biggest scoop of all time. The story of the red tape murders was splashed across the front page in type that, for size and blackness, had seldom been equalled. And below the glaring headlines was Peter Ashton's dramatic story of the arrest of Emily Gamble, complete with a photograph of Detective-Superintendent Budd of Scotland Yard.

The *Mail* came out with another scoop a few days later, when it disclosed that the body of Herbert Renshaw, the man who had escaped from Broadmoor eighteen months previously, had been found in a disused culvert in a wood near the asylum. He was still dressed in the tattered remnants of the postman's uniform.

'He must've crawled in there to avoid the searchers,' commented Mr. Budd, 'an' got wedged somehow. Poor feller.'

'I wonder why they didn't find 'im before,' said Leek.

'Most likely because they was lookin' for a live man,' answered Mr. Budd. 'Well, you did a good job o' work for once in yer life. I s'pose you'll want a year's rest ter get over it?'

'I could do with a bit o' time off,'

admitted Leek. 'You know, you'd've solved this red tape business a lot quicker if you'd listened ter me.'

'What d'you mean?'

'If you remember, I wanted to 'ypnotise Emily Gamble when we was first goin' to question 'er. If you'd've let me, she'd've confessed.'

Mr. Budd made no comment, but the look he gave the unfortunate Leek was eloquent.

GRIM DEATH
MURDER IN MANUSCRIPT
THE GLASS ARROW
THE THIRD KEY
THE ROYAL FLUSH MURDERS
THE SQUEALER
MR. WHIPPLE EXPLAINS
THE SEVEN CLUES
THE CHAINED MAN
THE HOUSE OF THE GOAT
THE FOOTBALL POOL MURDERS
THE HAND OF FEAR
SORCERER'S HOUSE
THE HANGMAN
THE CON MAN
MISTER BIG
THE JOCKEY
THE SILVER HORSESHOE
THE TUDOR GARDEN MYSTERY
THE SHOW MUST GO ON
SINISTER HOUSE
THE WITCHES' MOON
ALIAS THE GHOST
THE LADY OF DOOM
THE BLACK HUNCHBACK

We do hope that you have enjoyed reading this large print book.

Did you know that all of our titles are available for purchase?

We publish a wide range of high quality large print books including:
Romances, Mysteries, Classics General Fiction Non Fiction and Westerns

Special interest titles available in large print are:
The Little Oxford Dictionary Music Book, Song Book Hymn Book, Service Book

Also available from us courtesy of Oxford University Press:
Young Readers' Dictionary (large print edition) Young Readers' Thesaurus (large print edition)

For further information or a free brochure, please contact us at:
Ulverscroft Large Print Books Ltd., The Green, Bradgate Road, Anstey, Leicester, LE7 7FU, England.
Tel: (00 44) 0116 236 4325
Fax: (00 44) 0116 234 0205

PERFECT PIGEON

Richard Wormser

Easy come, easy go . . . That's the life of con men who stay one step ahead of the law, two steps ahead of each other. At twenty-three, Mark Daniels embezzled his way to a cool quarter million. Sure, he got caught; that was part of his plan. All he had to do was sit tight until he could safely grab his dough. Six years later, newly released from prison, he's got his chance — but then into his lap drops the loveliest woman in the world, with the slickest murder frame he's ever seen . . .

THE VAMPIRE MAN

Gerald Verner

Conway Jackson, amateur criminologist, receives a disturbing letter from his uncle, Sir James Gleeson, informing him that he feels himself to be in terrible danger, and imploring him to come to his country manor. Unfortunately, the letter has taken some time to reach him, and it shows unmistakable signs of having been steamed open. On his arrival, Jackson learns that his uncle was found strangled in his bedroom the night before — by what appears to be an inhuman monster that is destined not to stop at a single victim . . .

MANHATTAN BOMBSHELL

Norman Firth

Reporter Larry O'Halloran has got himself a great scoop. So he's shocked when his editor refuses to run it — and no rival newspaper will touch it, either. It seems the press in this city is caught in a stranglehold, scared to print the truth, fearing retribution from a mysterious figure named 'the Raven'. So Larry starts his own paper, the *Manhattan Bombshell*, printing the stories no other sheet dares to. But the Raven will make him pay for his audacity . . .

THE LATE MRS. FIVE

Richard Wormser

Soon after Paul Porter arrives in the small rural town of Lowndesburg, he is shocked to see his beautiful ex-wife Edith getting into an expensive limousine. He discovers she is now married to rich landowner John Hilliard the Fifth, to whose mansion he makes a visit hoping to sell agricultural machinery, only to find nobody home. But the local police know of his visit — and when they discover Edith's dead body there, he becomes the prime suspect as the slayer of the late Mrs. Five!

LORD JAMES HARRINGTON AND THE SPRING MYSTERY

Lynn Florkiewicz

James and his wife Beth are hosting the annual spring fair when wealthy recluse Delphine Brooks-Hunter is murdered. While James is summoned to the reading of her will and is tasked with solving an intriguing riddle, Beth tackles her own mystery after discovering a homeless man suffering from amnesia. As they delve deeper, a number of questions emerge. What links Delphine to the fairground folk? Who would harm such a refined lady? Are rumours of wartime espionage true? As they unravel the truth, they uncover more than they bargained for . . .